Nullarbor Pearl

Sarah Rossetti

Glass House Books
Brisbane

Dr. Sarah Rossetti lives in Perth, WA and in Uki in Northern NSW. In 1988, she completed a Bachelor of Arts with a Creative writing major, earning a Distinction in Communication & Cultural Studies at Curtin University. She has credits in a wide variety of genres and has won five national awards for screenwriting. Sarah writes commissioned TV dramas and feature documentaries, works as a script editor and assessor, and has lectured in screenwriting at three WA universities, and at SAE in Byron Bay, NSW. In 2007, Sarah was appointed board member of the Australian Writers' Guild, a position she held for three years. In 2009, she completed her PhD in Media Studies at Murdoch University, WA. *Nullarbor Pearl* is Sarah's debut novel, which she believes could easily to be adapted into a feature film, by enhancing her early film script with the novel's further development.

Don't let misunderstandings ruin your life.
– Dr. Sarah Rossetti

Glass House Books
an imprint of IP (Interactive Publications Pty Ltd)
Treetop Studio • 9 Kuhler Court
Carindale, Queensland, Australia 4152
sales@ipoz.biz
http://ipoz.biz/shop
First published by IP in 2024
© 2024, Sarah Rossetti (text) and IP

Printed in 16 pt Avenir Book on Caslon Pro 12 pt.

ISBN: 9781922830647 (PB) 9781922830654 (eBook)

A catalogue record for this book is available from the National Library of Australia

Written with the support of:

Contents

Acknowledgements

Book design: David P Reiter
Cover images: Graeme Miles Richards
Author photo: Wayne Brown

Much gratitude to the folk in two writing groups I belonged to while adapting the *Nullarbor Pearl* script into a novel. In UKI, NSW, these writers offered me great early feedback to expand my punchy, abbreviated script writing style into descriptive prose: Megan Albany, Holly Norton, Jandra Faranda, Tina Wilson, Lisa Stiffen and Bryan McClelland. In Perth, WA, group members Cathy Brown, Jennifer Burke and Mark Rous offered their feedback. Special thanks to Mark Dyer and Rita La Bianca, who rigorously advised me on chapters as they emerged and Christine Betcher for proof reading.

Early on, Fiona Johnson provided preliminary edits of the novel. My heartfelt thanks must go to Dr. David Reiter, my publisher, and his editor, Emma-Clare Daly, who attended to all of the final edits.

Prior to the novel's acceptance for publication, I asked a variety of readers for feedback, and was chuffed that older readers loved it just as much as young ones: Trsitan Kewe, Joan Keeling, Kerry Noonan, Beverley Costello, Gian Tentori, Catherine Fisher, Shanaz Lambat, Shiree Johnston, Valery Niazov, Peter Udinga, Rob Doria, Louise Ratcliffe, Sally Dietzler, David Young, Laura Richards, Chloe Traicos and Laurie De Pledge. Thanks to my sister, Donna Williams and dear old dad, Patrick Kontze, for their true, not too flattering, feedback. Thank you Gary Roberts, Brendan Varka and Kym James for encouraging me after reading an early draft, and Sharyn Clarke, Colin Thompson and Matheos Vandoros for feedback on the final copy.

I offer my enormous gratitude to Graeme Miles Richards, for creating the novel's striking cover designs, and to Wayne Brown for taking my portrait.

Finally, my heartfelt thanks to WA proud Noongar woman, Marianne Yoorgabilya Mackay, who offered suggestions and feedback on our agreed auspice that nothing secret would be revealed. She helped me write my way around First Nations learning that I never needed to know, as such deep learning is purposely missing from this magic realist work of fiction, for reasons that you are about to discover.

Foreword

Nullarbor Pearl has a long history. It began life as this poem, written in 1997: my early imaginings as a beginner poet, attaining my B.A. in Creative Writing at Curtin University, Western Australia.

> At closing time she grabs a tea towel
> and heads for the wheeze and gurgle
> of the aquarium,
> leans over it to wipe fingerprints.
>
> The smell of ocean shocks her absent skin
> like a reprisal.
> She reaches in to touch the seaweed,
> webs her fingers with it,
> glances at the door,
> takes a breath,
> and plunges,
> all of her face into the tank.
>
> A sea-horse glides down her nose,
> sweeps the dust from her smile.
> The smallest inmate nibbles
> her spinifex eyebrows.
> A truckie slaps the side glass.
> She leaps
> in a bubble-flurry of fins,
> wipes her face with the tea towel
> and runs behind the counter,
> giggling.

At that time, I was impressed by the work of emerging director, Christopher Watson, whom I offered the poem to, adding that I would write the short script for him to direct – if he could shoot it underwater. That ten minute film script, entitled *Pilbara Pearl*, rapidly made it into production with the support of Screenwest and Lotterywest, The Australian Film Commission, and the Pearl Consortium, directed by Christopher Watson and produced by Marian Bartsch and Karen Williams, then both working for Derek

Longhurst, at CVA Film and Television. Right away, they obtained an SBS presale and AFI distribution for the film. *Pilbara Pearl* went on to enjoy much success, screening on domestic and international TV networks and Qantas international flights, as well as on the big screen, picking up a swag of awards aided by brilliant performances by Bobbi Henry as Pearl and Christopher Pitman as Eddie. Readers of the novel may view the short film, *Pilbara Pearl*, via the link provided when you purchase the book.

Everybody who loved the short film urged me to write the feature film, so I set to work.

Once again, Screenwest and Lotterywest supported that initiative, funding three drafts of the feature film script, entitled *Nullarbor Pearl*, while Victor Gentile was their development officer. I was also given the opportunity to work in a script lab with Joan Scheckel in Los Angeles after I won an IF Award, as best emerging film maker in Australia. Back at home, I worked with Ken Kelso as the script editor of the first draft, with additional script advice from Jonathan Teplitzky and Martha Coleman. Deborah Parsons came on as script editor for the second draft, with Sally Ayre-Smith as producer. Sue Taylor came on in third draft, working closely with the script as Creative Producer, as well attending an Artista development program with me, but, despite all of this support, the film was not produced.

I decided that writing three drafts of *Nullarbor Pearl* as a film script was enough. I returned to study, this time to complete my PhD at Murdoch University, Western Australia, supervised by Associate Professors, Jennifer de Reuck and Mick Broderick. *Nullarbor Pearl* became the centre-piece script in a trilogy of 'Pearl' film scripts, written in tandem with my theoretical exegesis. That PhD, completed in 2008, was entitled, *Enigmatic Pearls: Authorship and Representation in Pilbara Pearl, Nullarbor Pearl and Showalwater Pearl.* Thanks must go to my daughter, Sophie Rossetti, for proofreading that PhD.

In addition to all of this collaborative assistance, my sincere thanks must go to my agent, Tim Curnow, who I cannot praise enough for his excellent service on all of my film projects over the decades.

Miraculously, I never tired of telling this tale and testing its veracity across all of these forms. In 2021, I decided to bring it to a readership as this novel, which was written with the support of the Department of Local Government, Sport and Cultural Industries, Western Australia.

Chapter One

The noonday sun burns Pearl's head through her frizzy brown hair as she splashes sky blue paint on a crumbling asbestos fence. She takes a step back, paintbrush in hand, liking how the ragged top of her 'mural' blends seamlessly with the cloudless sky. Pearl wonders how long it will be before old Piss-Pot-the-caretaker notices and tells her off. She glances past the mural to the Cockburn Cliff Caravan Park office, with its tattered curtains drawn. He'll be okay with her giving the driveway a lift, she hopes, as she uses her t-shirt to wipe the sweat off her top lip, but Mum? Different story.

Pearl works close to her mural so the power of it can't hit her like remembering does. Up close, it's just laid down colours that rests her mind rather than disturbs it.

Gutless, she thinks. A mural can be painted in bits, but you have to stand back to see if it works.

Pearl closes her eyes, takes a few big steps back and opens them. She likes that she got her cringe-worthy, adolescent dorkiness right, plus the excitement of beachcombing with a metal detector. She looks up at her freckle-faced dad, Big Red, who's giving her younger-self a lop-sided grin. Pearl can still feel the love in that grin and it kills her, like a punch she can't get out of the way of. Her heart flips as she remembers him singing to her that day as they hunted for treasure.

"You've got to get a bit of dirt on your hands, Pearl. You've got to get a bit of dirt on your hands. If you want to grow up to be a big, big lady, you've got to get a bit of dirt on your hands."

Pearl picks at the dried paint on her hand, wondering why she painted this. Because it felt like a puke trying to get out? Seeing Red in the mural reminds her that she doesn't even know who to *be* without him and painting this hasn't helped. No way could she paint what happened on the night of that treasure hunt, when he busted up with her mum, Marnie, after another one of their drunken brawls.

That paint's still too wet to touch, she tells herself, which doesn't stop her hearing the fight over and over in her dreams. Her kid-self never stops yelling her dreams into nightmares.

"Waaaaaaaaiit!" young Pearl wails at the back of her dad's ute until she runs out of air.

Pearl has tried, but she can't unsee his taillights burning down the main street, which left her feeling flatter than roadkill as she doubled over to vomit.

Looking down at the old spew stain on the driveway makes her blink back the sudden threat of tears. The gnawing question, that never stops gnawing, is how could he leave her stuck in this shit hole for the rest of her life? He used to send cash, care of Piss Pot so that Marnie wouldn't find out, and then nothing for years.

What am I? *Nothing?*

"You listening to me, Pearl?"

Pearl startles. No way she's letting Marnie catch her getting teary-eyed over Red. The paintbrush drips blue down her wrist. She steps forward and defiantly paints on.

"Paint over it I said!" Marnie yells from the driver's seat of her filthy Holden Kingswood.

She pushes her legs out of the car door, bending over belly bulge to lace up her battered white shoes with a cigarette dangling off her lip.

The caravan office curtains part. Piss Pot squints through, pulling his grey hair into a ratty ponytail. He comes out to look at the mural, bare feet planted apart. He rolls the cold frost off a can of Emu Bitter on his faded purple boardies, pulls the ring top open with a click and slurps a big gulp of beer.

Marnie wrestles out of her sedan seat and stands, calling out to Piss Pot as she marches over, "Don't worry. It'll be gone in no time."

Pearl yells over her shoulder, "Will not!"

Marnie eyes her child-endowment-cheating ex in the

painting with disgust.

She turns, giving Pearl the same filthy look as she spits out, "Why glorify a prick who doesn't even want to know ya?"

Gutted, Pearl angles away, glancing back at her dad in the painting with the corrugations of the fence now bending his face out of shape, thinking maybe she's right.

But his smile never lied.

Piss Pot sees her torment. "Bloody good likeness. Kid's got a gift," he slurs, burping beer fumes in Marnie's face. "Get to art school," he tells Pearl as he weaves his way back to 'work'.

Marnie snaps at his back, "Do you mind? I've got a hospital job lined up for her."

Pearl pushes down the urge to say something super bad, rising like acid in her throat.

She returns to her painting, ranting, "Not cleaning shitty bed pans. No way!"

Marnie stomps back to the Kingswood slinging the words out behind her like punches, "Yes you bloody will. Don't have to keep ya, now you're eighteen."

"Don't have to listen either."

Marnie halts, clenching her teeth as she resists the urge to swing around fast and stare down the fight in Pearl, but time's ticking and she's never been late for a hospital shift yet.

Hot anger erupts in Pearl because what she wants has never mattered one bit to either parent, especially not to Red.

She shrieks at Marnie's back, "I'll do what I bloody well like!"

Marnie slams the car door, shoves the key in the ignition, pumps the accelerator and finally gets the old rust bucket started on the third go. The Kingswood rattles alongside with cigarette smoke belching out the window and exhaust fumes out the back.

Marnie floors Pearl with her king hit, "Go on then, jump in the deep end and see what happens to ya. See if I care."

Hurt and hatred combust in Pearl as the Kingswood passes, kicking up dust on her freshly painted mural. Pearl throws the paintbrush at the back of the Kingswood and hits it, splattering a fan of blue on the dirty white boot with a satisfying thud.

Marnie turns on to the stinking-hot main road and revs off to work like it never happened.

With her pulse hammering in her neck, Pearl decides that it's high time she found out about that deep end.

She yanks someone's towel off the line and runs flat out for the cliff, ripping off her t-shirt and throwing it and the towel behind her as she sprints for the edge in her red bikini top and boardies. Without a thought for all the swimming lessons she never had, Pearl jumps way out.

If birds can fly, so can I!

"*Haaaaaaahhhhh!*" Pearl yells with her arms flapping madly beside her.

The salty smell rushes up and hits her like a reprisal as she soars briefly, free as a flying fish, and then she stalls, arms and legs flailing, wild hair flying as she hurtles toward the sea.

It's not as if she's never thought about it. On thinking days, Pearl calculates that if she jumps out far enough, she won't hit the cliff. That is, if it's not blowing a strong sea breeze. On thinking days, she's pretty sure she'll drown if she doesn't hit the cliff, since she can't swim, so she instantly dismisses the idea as suicidal, insane. But today is not a thinking day.

Today is a do or die day.

Pearl smashes through the surface for the first time in her life. Through dazzling bubbles, she sees the nearby reef and flashing fish with her own cheeks bloated out in amazement like a puffer fish.

If frogs can swim, so can I!

Pearl frog kicks down, upside down, pushing the water aside with big bird arms. She clutches on to a lump of limestone to peer in the mouth of a cave. Her eyes widen as she spies a blue-green lobster on a ledge with its antennae twitching. A strand of seaweed tickles past her cheek in the surge, delighting Pearl, until a gut clench warns her that she's being watched. Still white knuckling the limestone, Pearl flashes a look behind her between her trailing legs and up toward the surface.

Nothing.

She peers into the cave again.

Slanted sunlight streams in from a hole in the top of the limestone at the back of the cave. Something shadowy is moving back there, drifting alarmingly closer. Pearl blinks, trying to make it go, believing that she must be hallucinating, but it keeps coming. Bug-eyed, she freezes as she sees that the shadow has a young woman's face offering her a scary see-through smile. It reaches for her with cold watery fingers to touch her arm.

What the?

Creeped out, Pearl recoils in startled disbelief. Goosebumps race up her arms as she pushes back, away from the shadow, with the cave now at arm's length.

Another gut-clench warns her that she's *still* being watched.

With her lungs screaming for air, Pearl flashes another look behind her.

A large Bronze Whaler shark, growing ever clearer, is steadily approaching.

Paralysed, Pearl screams, releasing the last of her air.

Inside the cave, the shadow woman's expression darkens as it darts forward full pelt, coursing straight through Pearl's torso and out of her back to divert the shark.

Pearl jolts at the icy shock of its dark passage through her chest. She pulls her legs in under her and kicks off the reef, rocketing up doing frantic bird frog through sunbeams and a flashing school of silver anchovies. Swimming at lightning speed, they form a dizzying, dazzling ball around her as she rises.

Pearl breaks the surface, gasping, dispersing the fish above her. The spinning anchovy ball reforms and tornadoes off behind her, leaving Pearl confronted by blue sky and the sweaty face of an old fisherman with white zinc on his nose.

He leans further out of his listing dinghy full of flapping fish to reach for her, yelling, "Here! Quick!"

Pearl reaches for his hand but can't bird frog close enough with one arm out; worse, she rapidly starts to sink.

Alarmed, the fisherman grabs an oar and smacks it on the water behind her, yelling, "Gorn! Get out ya bastard!"

Pearl spins around, gasping as the shark fin surfaces a few metres behind her, undeterred by the spinning anchovies. She grabs the oar and the fisherman hauls her into the dinghy, almost capsizing it.

Pearl pulls her feet inside the rocking dinghy as the Bronze Whaler cruises alongside, easily as big as the boat. She silently slides below its black, beady eye-line to hide in the sludgy bottom with the half-dead Bream.

Pumped, the fisherman yanks the outboard motor chord, cussing, "Too fuckin' close for comfort!" as they roar for the shore. He eyes Pearl cowering in the bottom of the boat and barks questions at her, "You're Marnie's kid, aren't ya? Why the hell did you jump off that cliff?"

Pearl tries to sit up but can't get her ragged breathing under control. She reaches for the sides of the dinghy to pull herself up, but her hands are shaking too much.

Noticing, the fisherman speeds for the caravan park boat ramp, softening his tone as he says, "Just promise you'll never do that again."

Pearl raises her eyes and nods. No way she's going there again. Not now that she knows what's on the other side of all Mum's madness.

"Thanks, life saver," she says as she clambers out of the dinghy on shaky legs.

Grateful that her heart has stopped thumping, Pearl heads up the beach toward the caravan park as the fisherman throws his now lifeless catch in a bucket. As soon as his back is turned in the departing dinghy, she scampers up the cliff track.

*

There, Pearl sits on the towel with her legs over the edge, calves pressed hard against the cliff face. She leans forward, squinting past the white caps into the dark blue depths where the cave must be. The sea breeze has risen, blowing her damp curls back from her face. Waves pound the base of the cliff like distant drums. Pearl fancies that she sees the shark and the shadow still facing off in the depths. She shudders and straightens, to pull her red t-shirt back on. Pearl looks down at her chest and rubs the space between her breasts. No matter how hard she rubs, it doesn't warm the chilled feeling where the shadow darted through.

What the fuck just swam through me?

She hugs her knees to her chest and pushes up to stand and scream at the ocean as she backs away, "I'm not afraid of either of ya!" because she is, terrified of them both. She snatches up the towel and strides back toward the caravan park, calling behind her, "Just keepin' ma distance."

*

Back in her annexe, Pearl keeps chanting to try to feel safe, "Not afraid of ya, just keepin' ma distance," like it's true.

She pulls on some jeans and shoves clothes, brushes and paints into a rucksack, all of her paintings into a folio and her pet goldfish, Curly, into a jar of water from his tank. Worried that he might suffocate, she stabs holes in the lid with her paint-splodged Stanley blade.

"Bad news travels fast," Marnie announces as she flips back the tattered canvas flap of the annexe, pinning startled Pearl with an unflinching look. "What did I tell ya? You're lucky to be *alive*."

Pearl needs no convincing. She hefts the rucksack on her right shoulder, tucks her art folio under her left arm and picks up the jar with Curly in it.

"Going somewhere?" Marnie asks warily. She grabs the free strap on Pearl's backpack demanding to know, "What'd you see in that water?"

"Going to Aunty Beryl's," Pearl replies, wrenching her backpack strap out of Marnie's clutches. "No sharks, no shitty bed pans, no you."

Marnie recoils at this living proof of the dread that never leaves her.

"Knew you'd piss off one day. Like father, like daughter."

Pearl hears the hurt in Marnie's voice and shoulders past, trying not to listen to her ranting, "Rushed home to check on ya, and this is all the thanks I get for keeping you safe *all ya life*? Why the bloody Nullarbor? Just 'cause you were born there, won't fix anything. Does Beryl know you're coming?"

Feeling safer outside, Pearl turns to Marnie.

"Don't have to ask – she loves me," she answers with more conviction than she feels, unaware of how the stark sunlight on her face reveals her own pain.

Marnie's face closes shop. "Do you good, a stint in the desert," she says in her flattest voice. "Do me good, too. Make sure you pull your weight, my girl. Least you could do since that place's gunna be yours one day."

"One day when they're dead," Pearl mutters as she turns away.

Marnie sees a mother-of-pearl necklace glinting out of the top of Pearl's t-shirt and calls after her, "Hey! Give that back. That's Nana's necklace!"

Pearl flicks Marnie a last messed up look as she jogs toward the road, calling behind her, "Time it got handed down."

Too defeated to argue the toss, Marnie calls back, "You'll be sorry."

She pulls a packet of cigarettes out of her nurse's uniform pocket with shaking fingers.

Lighting up, Marnie draws back deeply and exhales, adding quietly, "Never meant it, 'bout the deep end. Always said, stay out of the water. But no. What bloody good did it do ya? Any of us?"

She sadly eyes happy Red and Pearl off prospecting in Pearl's mural with a hole in her heart so deep because she's lost them both now. Marnie steps back into the annexe, sits on Pearl's bed and sobs.

Chapter Two

Far from the coast now, Pearl slides low in her bus seat, with her brown knees exposed through ripped jeans. She hopes that focusing on Curly – in the netting behind the seat in front – sloshing in his jar, will hypnotise her blues away. Her rucksack is jammed beside her, barring the other mostly old fart passengers from getting anywhere near her.

Failing Curly hypnosis, Pearl closes her eyes and tries to sleep, to stop replaying Marnie's abuse about her glorifying a prick who doesn't even want to know her, which now feels painfully true. Staring at the back of her eyelids only amplifies her remorse.

Mum was right. Both of them abandoned her – like father, like daughter.

It's keeping Pearl awake as the cool air-conditioned bus rumbles ever eastward toward the Nullarbor desert through the shimmering heat of the day.

Despite knowing that she'll get an earful, Pearl pulls out her mobile to call Marnie, but there's no service. She desperately wants to make a new start, but her parents' last drunken fight still plays relentlessly in her head. Pearl squirms lower in her bus seat, defenceless.

"If a man can't take his own daughter for a swim, what's the fuckin' use of living at the beach?"

"Where else could we afford near the hospital? If you got off your arse and got a real job instead of pissing off prospecting all the time, we could live where we bloody well like. And believe me, Red; I want to live anywhere but here."

"Who could blame a man for getting away from a crazy, over-protective cow like you? The kid needs to learn how to *swim!*"

In her annexe, young Pearl pulls her pillow around her ears. It doesn't muffle the sound of the door of the caravan slamming, nor Red hurling his prospecting gear into the back of his utility, again.

She throws off her bedding as she hears Marnie storming out after him, yelling, "You piss off one more time and there's no coming back."

"Deal!" Red bellows as he starts up the ute and revs it.

Young Pearl leaps out of bed, but it's too late. He's already roaring off for the last time.

She runs up the dark driveway as his taillights burn on to the main street, wailing,

"Waaaaaaaaiit!"

Unable to bear it any longer, Pearl opens her eyes and squirts water from her drink bottle on her face, drying it with her t-shirt. It catches on a sharp bit in the mother-of-pearl necklace. She pulls the neck of her t-shirt away from the necklace like she needs air, and she does.

Pearl sucks in a big breath and slowly, silently sighs it out, which makes her feel marginally better. She stares out of the window at the old mine shafts and the roadside water pipe snaking through Goldfields of endless yellow grass, wondering if her dad's still out there prospecting.

*

During the night, Pearl wakes in the foetal position, curled against the window, with a gasping yelp that saves her from the shadow dragging her out of the sea cave into the open jaws of the shark. Despite the cool air, she's wet with sweat and, once again, she uses her t-shirt to wipe her face. Again, it gets snagged on something sharp in the necklace. She pulls it off to take a closer look.

The first thing she did after getting back from the cliff was snatch it out of Marnie's jewellery box because she was never allowed to wear it, or even play with it, as a kid. Pearl stares at the necklace, beginning to understand why. She runs her fingers over the jagged shark tooth centrepiece and shudders at the hole it has torn in her damp red t-shirt.

*

Pearl wakes exhausted at dawn and rubs her face as the bus pulls over, its gears grinding down.

A blinking push bike light lumbers past with lumpy brown saddle bags, ridden by a Japanese cyclist. He pauses to take in the wide main street's ghost town buildings. He pulls over, longingly eyes the headlights of the bus as he removes his helmet, squirts water from his bottle over his face, and turns to gape at the wide main street's ghost town buildings.

Pearl blinks, wondering if she's still dreaming. Nobody *sane* attempts to ride a pushbike across the scorching Nullarbor desert in summer, but this little Japanese cyclist looks ready to die trying.

The middle-aged bus driver, Clarrie, announces into his microphone, "Coolgardie. Oldest mining town in the West."

Below Pearl's window, a huge windmill blade is disappearing into one of the bus's open luggage compartments. The lid is slammed shut, offering Pearl her first glimpse of a well-built, blonde hunk, who just stashed the windmill blade in the hold.

Surely not. She blinks to make absolutely sure that he is actually getting on her bus full of transport discounted retirees, except for herself of course. As the hunk straightens, his shoulder muscles ripple beneath his tight blue t-shirt, above the promise of perfect pecs. His slim hips, accentuated by tight jeans with a big belt buckle over a flat stomach, have Pearl inwardly wolf whistling.

And then she sees it: in her reflection in the window, her frizzy brown hair has piled up alarmingly high on the side of the window from sleeping against it, like a bad beret in a high wind. She tugs her fingers through it to try and flatten the mess, praying that hunkalicious doesn't look up and see her, like some chick pulling her hair out 'cause he's so hot.

His good-messy, blonde hair and something shiny on a leather strap around his neck are glinting in the relentlessly rising sun, the heat of the day fast approaching.

Pearl instantly regrets not taking a shower before Marnie barged in because now her hair has a fishy smell from hiding in the bottom of the dinghy. If she showered, she would have changed her pongy, ripped t-shirt too, she thinks, as he looks up and sees her eyeing him up.

Look away. Look at anything but him.

Pearl scratches through her rucksack looking for her favourite strawberry perfume, but it's too late. He's already walking along the bus aisle toward her. She self-consciously grabs Curly's jar out of the webbing on the back of the seat in front to focus on him, rather than the hunk.

"Morning," he says, smiling as he stashes his duffle bag and takes the empty seat across from her.

Pearl notices his perfect white teeth as she gives him a quick nod and then she focuses back on Curly. As the bus pulls out, she sees one of her seascape paintings half out of her folio, wedged between her seat and the side of the bus. When she tries to yank it out, it rips.

"Fuck," she mutters. "I loved that painting."

Pearl stashes Curly's jar back in its webbing, wrestles the bus window open and throws the ripped seascape out the window, followed by the rest of her ocean paintings, like bad omens best forgotten. She glances at the surprised hunk, but their gaze is broken by the old bat, female co-driver, marching down the aisle toward them.

"What'd you think you're doing?" she demands, in spitting distance from Pearl's face.

"What's it look like?" Pearl retorts, jutting her chin at the paintings blowing down the street.

"Littering," the old bat snaps as she leans across Pearl and slams her window shut. "Stop it or get off."

As she strides back up the front, Pearl jabs at the air behind the old bat's back with a raised middle finger.

Amused, the hunk leans into the aisle to joke with Pearl, "Know what you just did? You brought water to the desert."

Pearl smiles and pulls out Curly's jar. She inserts a straw through one of the Stanley blade holes in the top, almost drinking instead of blowing air into it. Curly bounces happily in the bubbles as Pearl gazes out at the treeless, dust-dry limestone plains, speckled with low, grey-blue clusters of Saltbush.

"Ninety mile straight," Clarrie announces. "Australia's longest, straightest bit of road."

*

In the heat of the day, as the bus relentlessly crosses the desert on the numbingly boring highway, Pearl takes advantage of the hunk going to the rear toilet to dig for her strawberry perfume in her rucksack. She sprays it on her hair just in time. As the toilet door opens, she zips the perfume back into her rucksack, grabs a pencil and the last sketch in her folio – Big Red as a prospector beside a mine shaft – drawing on it like she just dashed it off.

What's taking him so long?

Pearl glances back and jumps as she sees him peering over her shoulder. She hastily stashes the sketch under her seat.

"What'd you do that for?" he asks.

"Cause it's crap."

He lingers, eyeing the dried paint on her t-shirt. "Looked pretty good to me. Are you an artist?"

Pearl shrugs with a twinge of excitement 'cause she's sure it wasn't the paint he was checking out.

"I'm Eddie," he says, eyeing the seat beside her. "Mind if I sit here?"

Pearl gives him an almost imperceptible nod, like, 'suit yourself, yeah, if you like', but her gut's clenching with so much excitement that she can't trust herself to sound casual.

He hefts her rucksack and stashes it in the hatch above.

As he slides into the seat beside her, Pearl sees spinifex blowing down the dusty highway, reminding her of the old Westerns that she and Red used to watch when she was little.

"It was all an ocean once," Eddie says near her ear.

Pearl glances at him, for the first time noticing playful suggestiveness in his dark blue eyes and a cute little constellation of freckles across his nose.

"Better like this," she mutters. "No sharks."

Eddie's eyes widen with amusement.

He pulls Curly's jar from the netting and waggles him at Pearl, making *Jaws* movie noises, "Ner nur. Ner nur."

Funny. Not.

He unscrews Curly's jar to check him out. Pearl notices what was glinting in the sun around his neck: a gold nugget the size of a cherry, hanging off a leather strap.

"You a prospector?"

"Nah. I fix windmills."

He stretches his leg to get his hand down the front pocket of his oh-so-tight jeans and withdraws a small white shell, which he drops in Curly's jar. Plink.

Curly goggles at it like he likes it.

"There you go, buddy," Eddie says as he screws the lid back on.

"Funny looking oyster shell," Pearl reckons with a flirty little smile, which is completely lost on Eddie as he passionately launches into his favourite subject.

"Prehistoric, they reckon. I was gobsmacked when that shell came up the first time I sunk a windmill bore. Plenty more 'round here like it, too."

"Bore water? Out here?"

"Rainwater seeps through the ancient limestone," Eddie enthuses, "and goes into this giant underground sea."

He gazes at Pearl's necklace, adding, "That's amazing. Where'd you get *that*?"

"Handed down from my great-grandma, but I never knew her. Her name was Pearl, same as me."

"Good name, Pearl," he replies, extending a hand to shake.

Their gaze meets for an electric moment as their hands clasp but forget to shake. Curly madly starts wagging his tail at Eddie, distracting them.

"Ha!" Pearl exclaims, withdrawing her hand. "He likes ya."

Eddie's instantly attracted to the little crease above Pearl's generous lips, the almond shape of her hazel eyes, her great tan and sun-bleached, wild hair, all signalling hell yes fun. Then how come she's shy? he wonders, taking in her fit, tom-boy build, until he notices her, noticing him noticing…

Eddie looks down at Curly, offering Pearl the chance to sneak a good look at his profile. She likes the earthy natural smell of him, the square, decisive set of his jaw and his freckles remind her of Red, in a good way. She wonders how old he is – maybe five years older – all man, compared to the boys who usually go for her.

Thank God school's out.

Eddie's blue-eyed gaze tracks back to Pearl's necklace and up to the green flecks in her eyes, captivated.

*

Later that night, when the bus lights are dimmed for sleeping, Pearl and Eddie share a two litre Coke bottle which Eddie tops up with a half bottle of rum. They are careful to keep it well below the driver's eye-line.

"Why'd you come here?" he asks, slurring a little as Pearl takes her seventh swig of warm rum and Coke.

"Had nuff ocean."

"Yeah, reckon," Eddie agrees as he nudges Curly's jar with his knee. "Fish fuck in it."

"Not Curly," Pearl slurs back, "He's a fresh water little fucker."

"Me, too."

Eddie drapes his gold nugget necklace around Curly's jar to distract the gaping goldfish.

"You from around here?" Pearl asks.

"Nah."

"So, where's home? Perth?"

"Cervantes," he mutters. "Haven't been back for years."

Pearl sees how conflicted about that he is, and waits.

Eddie gives her a direct look and decides just to tell her.

"Dad died three years ago. Six months later Mum swam out to sea and didn't swim back."

Pearl opens her mouth and forgets to shut it, amazed that anyone could share such a huge secret with no shame.

"I'm sorry to hear that, Eddie," she blurts out a little too forcefully, because everybody says that don't they? Without looking away, she exhales, feeling for him, adding, "God. How'd you deal with *that*?"

Eddie sees the sincerity in Pearl's eyes. He likes that she's straight up like him, not just curious and pretending to care like some people he used to call friends.

He shuffles in his seat, but can't get comfortable, wondering why he's risking scaring her off, thinking maybe the rum is talking. Plus, they may never see each other again, but that's not it. Eddie feels that he could say almost anything to this gorgeous girl, and she wouldn't judge him.

"Just been knocking around fixing windmills," he admits, too wowed to continue.

Pearl nods, understanding only too well. For the same reason: that they may never see each other again, she confides, "Been pretty messed up myself. Dad ran off when I was twelve, 'cause Mum's a bossy bitch, angry all the time and fuckin' crazy. Had to get away from her," she adds, looking into his eyes.

This time their gaze holds: Pearl recognises the pain in him, so like her own. Mortified that she might have hit a raw nerve, she impulsively kisses Eddie on the lips.

Surprised, he tenses like a coiled spring.

Stupid.

She begins to pull back, but he gently takes her face in his big hands and kisses her back, softly at first, and with rising intensity as their tongues meet and entwine.

Pearl realises with astonishment that she's never been kissed so perfectly before.

Who is this guy?

She returns his kisses with equal passion as her desire ignites and races south, making her thighs tremble.

With only thin t-shirts and denim between their naked skin, they kiss and caress even more urgently, oblivious to the snores of nearby passengers.

Pearl can't stop herself from making blissful little sighs.

Eddie's utterly wowed because she feels so right, so bloody perfect, but she's making sounds! He pulls out of the kiss and reaches up to gently cover her mouth, as the other hand slides under her t-shirt to feel her perfect nipples hardening beneath her bikini top.

Neither notices his gold nugget necklace falling to the floor.

Upfront, Clarrie elbows the off-duty female driver awake with a jut of his chin toward the back.

Torch in hand, she quietly walks down the aisle and snaps on the torch in Pearl's enraptured face.

Clarrie turns up the lights, causing gasps and groans from the sleepy passengers.

Pearl and Eddie jolt upright in their seats as the old bat marches forward and grabs the microphone, announcing, "Sorry for the bright lights, ladies and gents, but there's two young passengers up the back who think this is a hotel room."

All the passengers crane their necks, zeroing in on red-faced Pearl and Eddie with shocked whispers.

"That's right," the old bat adds, smirking into the microphone, "It's a bus, kids."

Shame!

Pearl and Eddie look at each other in the bright light and almost laugh with sexually charged, rebellious ridiculousness.

Eddie leaps up, pulls on the chord to stop the bus and grabs his duffle bag and Pearl's rucksack.

Pearl rescues Curly's jar out of the seat pouch in front. She sees Eddie's gold nugget glinting on the floor beneath it and snatches it up as she rushes off the bus behind him.

The passengers stare down their noses from their high windows at Pearl and Eddie as Clarrie opens the luggage compartment for Eddie to retrieve his windmill blade.

The bus rumbles back on to the highway, clouding them in ochre dust.

Pearl and Eddie laugh as they dump their stuff and brush themselves off, but once the dust settles, there's a new awkwardness between them.

Eddie casts his hand at the windmill back off the road, saying, "Don't worry. We're not going to die of thirst. Only sunk that bore a couple of months ago."

They walk toward the moonlit windmill and high tank stand in silence, both amazed at the intensity of what just happened.

Way too fast.

Pearl silently hands Eddie his nugget necklace.

"Thanks," he says, pulling it over his head. "Glad one of us was thinking."

He moves towards Pearl, but she pulls back, poker faced, her mind already doing double time shame.

How could I be that piss-weak, falling for the first hunk who knows how to kiss?

Eddie frowns, uncomprehending, but then he smiles good-naturedly as he takes the empty bottle from her rucksack and goes to refill it at the low water tank tap, along with his empty Coke bottle.

"It's not that I don't like you, Eddie," Pearl calls after him in a ridiculously high voice that makes her cringe, "Just got a lot of stuff to sort out."

Eddie ambles back, hands back her filled water bottle, stashes the Coke bottle in his duffle bag and lets her know, "My ute's up the road, not far. Left it on the job."

He hefts the duffle bag and starts walking.

Pearl doesn't follow.

Eddie turns, saying, "Let's just get you to a roadhouse. There's an old one only a couple of clicks this way, nice people. Or there's the big new one not much further on that's been hiring lately."

Pearl sits on her rucksack, "Fine here, thanks," she stalls.

She's not one bit ready for the world to turn again, and she's definitely not sure what she feels, except totally turned on and confused.

Eddie understands how hot they got and getting sprung was enough to freak anyone out, but this?

He wonders if she's all there, and it shows as he asks, "*What?*"

Pearl notices and thinks he's probably right, since she just jumped off a cliff, but her mind is made up, so whatever it takes.

She gazes down the road as if precious freedom flows in both directions and tells him, "Just gunna go whichever way the wind blows."

Unhappily resigned, Eddie starts backing away, offering her a gaze full of mischief and maddening understanding. Pearl looks him over, utterly attracted.

"Okay," he replies, taking another step back, "take care."

He makes a show of picking up the huge windmill blade with muscled ease.

"I'd ask for your number, but there's no reception out here," he teases, giving her the benefit of his dazzling smile, adding infuriatingly, "If you ever want to find me, break the windmill."

Pearl gives him the thumbs up, pretending massive indifference, "Huh. Bye, Eddie."

A crow lands on the dawn-lit windmill. Its 'fark fark' call grates on Pearl as she watches Eddie striding down the road, getting smaller and smaller as he nears the horizon. The rising sun glints off his windmill blade, making her see spots. Pearl rubs her eyes and glances up the road in both directions. She jogs behind the windmill urgently unzipping her jeans and squats to pee.

A red Australia Post van roars into view, pumping eighties Melbourne punk music.

"*Waaaaaaaaiit!*" Pearl yells, dragging up her jeans as she races back to the road, but the postman doesn't notice her waving her arms above her head in his rear-view mirror.

She watches his rear lights blending with the hot sun rising on the horizon with dismay.

Pearl takes a few gulps of weird-tasting windmill water, throws the bottle at the cussing crow, pulls a scribbled mud map from her pocket, and squints at it. She tries to concentrate on the map, but her thoughts return to Eddie.

She doesn't know why she pushes guys away, but it's always the same and, every time she does, a little bit of her hope goes with them. She rips more denim out of the knee of her jeans, wondering if she'll ever get the guts to go all the way with any of them. They think she's so fast, but she's as slow as a wet week – and it feels so familiar – the wrench of watching them go, just like her dad and that part of her heart that went with him.

With a sharp intake of breath, Pearl realises that she left her Red-at-the-mine-shaft sketch under her bus seat, which makes her wonder if that's a curse or a blessing. Is life trying to tell her that it's high time she left him behind, or just miserably reminding her that he's gone, and he wants to stay gone?

Chapter Three

Pearl trudges along the hot highway. Shading her eyes, she stops, staring up in amazement at the size and grace of a Wedge-tailed Eagle taking off into the sun, making its outline glow. Its massive wings easily span the broad width of highway with its brown wing tips curving upward, like the fingers of a Balinese dancer.

A rising eagle in the rising sun must be a sign, she decides. Rising above her family crap is a good thing, maybe even divine.

Then she sees the putrid kangaroo entrails dangling from its talons.

Well, maybe not divine. Her family aren't roadkill, and she hasn't ripped their guts out any more than they've ripped out hers, Pearl thinks defensively. She shifts the backpack straps on her shoulders and trudges on.

Every living thing has to eat, she tells herself, which just reminds her of how hungry she is. She passes the ripped open kangaroo carcass holding her nose, relieved that the wind is carrying most of its stench the other way.

Licking her dry lips, she regrets throwing her water bottle at the crow.

A bit further ahead, she sees an abandoned fridge on the other side of the road with 'Closed' painted on it. Is that Aunty's place, closed?

She hears an engine chugging. The noise is coming from a hot pink water tanker parked down the driveway beside a windmill, obscuring the main building.

On the scorching wind, she faintly hears Aunty Beryl's voice yelling, "Righto!"

Pearl beams and jogs across the highway toward her birthplace.

At the rundown roadhouse, the water pump shuts off. Beryl pulls the pink pipe out of the tank on the high stand beside the windmill. She catches the spillage in a watering can which she places at her feet. As she hangs the pipe high up on the back of the tanker, a little water splashes into her eyes.

Beryl stalls, like she's seen something, wipes her eyes and intently peers through the shimmering heat haze already rising off the highway.

"Aunty!" Pearl croaks with a dry throat as she makes out cuddly Aunty Beryl with her hands on her hips, in a too tight white t-shirt, denim shorts and thongs, peering in her direction.

Beryl's big bear of a partner, Yanush, pads out of the roadhouse barefoot in overalls, with a yellow post-it note stuck to his forehead, to see what Beryl's noticed on the highway. He hardly recognises this sliver of a girl jogging toward them with a rucksack bobbing on her back.

"She's here," Beryl tells him, peeling off his forehead the note which says 'Office Tart'. She pushes it into the bib of his overalls.

"Nothing wrong with your eyes, Bubba," he assures her. "Still better than mine."

Beryl shades her eyes with her hand to look up at the water truck cabin, calling, "Pay ya later, Pink." She casts a hand at the highway, adding, "Got family coming."

Pink leans out of the cabin in her pink peak cap, answering, "Stretching the friendship, begging for water you're too skint to pay for," but all of Beryl's attention is back on Pearl.

"Alright, alright," Pink mutters as she sees the backpacker fast approaching. "I'll pick it up on my way back to Perth."

"You're a gem," Beryl distractedly replies as she picks up her watering can.

She rounds the tanker and petrol pumps as Yanush gratefully reaches up to shake Pink's hand.

"Yeah, yeah," Pink mutters, withdrawing her hand to turn the wheel as she pulls out, with a pink wishing stone bracelet dangling off her wrist.

Pink hits the road, passing Pearl loping up the driveway.

Pearl smiles at the old roadhouse with its now faded, multi-coloured plastic strips flapping in the entrance. The ancient, round caravan is still parked up behind the windmill and the giant fish tank is past the pumps, where it used to be. They must have filled it with dirt to try and grow herbs in it, she thinks, but the plants look shrivelled up and dry.

Pearl wonders why her aunty's walking like a penguin, until she sees that she's trying not to spill a drop out of her watering can. Beryl carefully places the can between her feet and opens her arms for a hug. Yanush catches up as Pearl thumps down her rucksack.

She races over, ducks under her aunty's open arms to grab the watering can and drinks sideways from it, slopping water down her front. Yanush frowns at the spillage.

"Been expecting you," Beryl says, grinning. "Save some for the plants, luv."

Pearl wipes her mouth, "Did Mum call?"

"Nah, just knew."

"She's so grown up," Yanush tells Beryl.

"You've grown bigger too, Bear," Pearl replies, winking at his protruding belly.

Yanush makes a show of throwing her rucksack over his shoulder and padding back inside with it, straight-backed with his belly pulled in.

Pearl smiles, asking Beryl, "Is he getting ready to hibernate?"

Yanush overhears, calling behind him, "Don't listen, Bubba!"

Pearl wrinkles her nose. *Bubba?*

She takes Curly's jar out of the webbing in the side of her rucksack, unscrews the lid to offer him more air and places the jar on top of the herb garden. Curly swims backwards, away from the plastic orange fish he sees lying dead between the herbs.

They brush aside the plastic strips at the front door as Yanush drops Pearl's rucksack behind the servery counter. Beryl turns to get a good look at her niece.

"Is that Nana's necklace?" she asks, eyeing it hanging around Pearl's neck with distaste.

Pearl nods.

"Haven't seen that in years."

Beryl opens her arms again for that hug, but reels back, exclaiming, "Oh poh!" The smell gets worse as Pearl's arms rise, making Beryl hold her nose as she asks, "You been *fishin*?"

Pearl smiles, ducks aside and grabs the last Mars bar off the servery counter.

Yanush frowns, but Beryl waves his disapproval away.

"Ta, yum, starving," Pearl says with a caramelly grin.

"Walk the thousand kilometres, did ya?"

Pearl shakes her head, "Got kicked off the bus for drinking."

"Not wodka, I hope?" Yanush asks, amused.

"Rum."

Yanush's smile fades as he heads back into the office to sit at a desk strewn with bills, all with bright yellow overdue stickers on them. He rubs the grey stubble on his big square chin and pours a vodka, wondering if they will go to jail if the roadhouse doesn't sell.

Pearl stares at the puttied, half-painted walls, planks and ladders and ten litre tins of pale blue paint in the dining room. She pokes her head through the servery to check the kitchen wall, happy to see low horizontal pencil marks measuring her height on each birthday: 'Pearl 1' all the way up to 'Pearl 6'.

She ducks through to stand against the wall beside them, pushes her hand to the wall at the top of her head and turns to see, calling to Aunty as she enters, "Grown this much, eh?"

"Tall like your dad."

"You seen him?" Pearl asks, spinning back to face Beryl.

"I would have told ya, luv," Beryl assures her.

Pearl averts her disappointed gaze to the paint tins in the dining room, muttering, "Gunna be an artist."

"Still got all the paints and paper you left here," Beryl replies fondly, "stashed under the bed in the caravan."

Yanush calls from the office, "You can paint all you like, kid, as long as it's walls."

Pearl nods, asking, "How long have you been closed?"

"Even when we were open, hardly anyone came," Beryl

admits. "Can't compete with the cheap fuel at the new joint up the road."

She casts an arm in the opposite direction to the way Pearl came from.

"Not even one kilometre that way, fast food 'round the clock, staff coming out of their ears, nice rooms. They've got the bloody lot."

"Bastards!" Pearl curses as she yanks off her necklace and plonks it on the counter.

"We're getting the place ready to sell," Beryl mutters, so low that Pearl doesn't hear her with her head down, yanking a towel out of her rucksack.

She looks toward the sound of running water in the Ladies toilet and shower room.

Beryl stares at the shark tooth centrepiece in the necklace as Pearl races into the Ladies, rattling the sign on the door that says 'Short Showers Only'.

Pearl leans on the sink in the steamy bathroom to wrestle off her runners, knocking a bottle of prescription eye drops to the floor. She notices Beryl's name on it with a frown as she replaces it on the shelf.

Dragging down her jeans, she calls to the woman behind the shower curtain, "Hey you! Time to get out."

She throws the woman's towel over the shower rail while yanking off her t-shirt and kicking off her jeans, yelling, "Come on, quick!"

The water shuts off. Eddie opens the curtain with a towel around his slim hips, delighted to see Pearl kicking off her jeans with her head stuck in her t-shirt, offering him an unrestricted view of her skimpy red bikini.

"Need a hand?" he asks.

Pearl wrestles off her top, gaping at Eddie's broad, hairless chest and up into his amused gaze.

"Glad the wind blew you this way, Pearl. Did you ask them for a job?"

"Um listen, Eddie. Beryl's my aunty, so…"

"Full of surprises, aren't you?"

"So, we never met, okay? Just don't say anything."

Eddie looks into Pearl's tense gaze, not comprehending as he yanks his jeans off the hook. He drags them over his wet legs under his towel.

Commando hunk.

Pearl can't take her eyes off his tanned, perfect pecs flexing as he zips up his jeans, asking, "What'd you think I'd say?"

"Do you usually shower in the Ladies?"

"Only if it needs fixing," Eddie replies as he snatches up a wrench from the shower floor, the rest of his stuff off the toilet lid, and heads out.

Pearl pulls off her bikini and rushes into the shower, allowing herself a few moments to luxuriate with her eyes closed under the jets. She starts washing her hair with Beryl's shampoo, relaxing for the first time in days. She sighs, massaging the sweet apple smelling shampoo into her hair, but is soon jolted out of it by banging on the door.

"Move it, Pearl," Beryl calls from the dining room. "That's our drinking water!"

As Pearl hurriedly rinses the shampoo out, the door is thrown open by someone she can't see from inside the curtain. She snaps off the water and pulls her towel off the rail to her chest.

"No more showers 'til the windmill's fixed," Yanush growls as he exits, slamming the door.

*

"Lunch time," Beryl hollers up at the windmill, pushing aside the fly strips in the entrance.

Eddie gives her the thumbs up from the windmill platform and starts climbing down its ladder.

Beryl enters the kitchen and sees Pearl slavering at the two burgers-with-the-lot that Yanush has made for the four of them.

"Want me to cut them in half?" Pearl asks, hoping not.

Yanush grabs a couple of pea and ham soup cans from the

almost empty pantry.

"We're starting to look like hamburgers," he replies as he opens one of the cans and hands it to Beryl with a dessert spoon.

"Aren't you going to heat them up?"

"Too hot for hot," Beryl answers, wiping her forehead with a t-towel.

Talk about hot! Pearl tries not to stare through the servery at Eddie entering the dining room. He wiggles his eyebrows at her as he heads for the Gents to wash his hands.

"Sure you don't want the *Ladies*?" Pearl calls through. "What's your name, hottie?"

Eddie gives her his killer smile as he answers, "Eddie. And you are?"

"My eighteen-year-old niece, Pearl," Beryl replies, like 'end of conversation'.

Eddie's surprised. He would have put her at twenty-something.

"Back in a tick," he tells Yanush, who's heading into the office.

Beryl gives Pearl a stern look as Eddie enters the Gents.

Pearl elbows her, whispering, "Is he a ten or what?"

Beryl gives in to a grin, holding ten fingers up, which is not lost on Yanush, returning with his vodka.

"Good worker – for an Aussie," he tells Pearl, as he takes a red vinyl chair off one of the many white Formica tables pushed away from the walls in the dining room. "Bit cheeky, but plenty of pepper in his arse."

No doubt, Pearl imagines, as she grabs cold water and tumblers from the fridge.

Eddie heads out of the Gents as Beryl places his burger on the table.

Pearl's already started hers, making ferocious eating noises at him as she sits opposite, "Num yum".

The penny drops. Beryl lowers her soup can and spoon.

"What's with the 'what's your name,' eh?" she asks Eddie. "Ray might have dropped you off with the mail, but you had to be on the same bus. So, you *both* must have got kicked off for drinking."

Suppressing a smile, Eddie replies, "She's a good drinker, but I walk faster."

He turns to tell Yanush, who's busy eating his soup, "The new blade's in, but all the bolts are rusting through and need replacing."

"Add it to the list," Yanush says with a defeated sigh, reaching for his vodka. "Just oil 'em and we pay you for the blade and labour when we sell. That okay with you?"

Eddie waves it away. "Food and board's fine thanks, mate," he replies, glancing at Pearl, who suddenly stops munching on her burger. "Got nothing much else on… yet."

Pearl puts her burger down, pleasing Eddie, who's hoping that she has taken his hint as a sign that he wants to stay on for her, but she's staring at Beryl, asking, "What do you mean, *selling?*"

"Told you 'bout that new place up the road slaughtering us," Beryl reminds her.

"Capitalist monstrosity," Yanush mutters, pushing his empty soup can away.

Pearl frowns. She's never known them anywhere else.

"But it's been in the family forever, ever since Nana Raeleen," she begins, trailing off as she realises that it's never going to be hers now.

"Talk about it later, luv," Beryl mutters, glancing at Eddie and back at Pearl, who should know better: family talk's private.

Pearl rubs her eyes as she gulps down the last of her burger, asking, "Can I have a room out the back, please, Aunty? Too hot in the caravan. Need some serious sleep."

Beryl looks to Yanush, who nods and tells Pearl, "Right after we finish painting that wall."

Pearl goes behind the counter to pull her mobile from her backpack, strides into the kitchen and squats to take a selfie beside the 'Pearl 1-6' birthday pencil stripes that might be gone soon, but her good memories of growing up here won't.

*

The sun is beginning to set, casting burnt orange hues and ochre dust into Pearl's room. The hot breeze rhythmically sucks the threadbare curtains in and out of the grimy window, knocking dead flies off the sill and letting live ones in.

Pearl imagines a sleeping dragon, but she's barely able to keep her eyes open. She crawls on to the cigarette-holed, chenille bedspread with a half-eaten chip bun, too tired to wash the paint off her hands or brush her teeth for the second time that day. She thinks of Eddie hunkalicious in the next room and dismisses it 'cause there's way bigger fish to fry.

Sadness swamps her as she thinks about how much older Aunty and Yanush look with their hair turning grey. It must be the stress of not being able to keep their heads above water.

It takes her back to growing up here, getting baths out the front in the fish tank without a care in the world that her butt was exposed to every motorist who pulled in for fuel. All her mum cared about was keeping Pearl's head above the surface, because the tank was so deep, so she said. Pearl can still feel the rough, wet flannel scrubbing her face and behind her ears. She smiles, remembering how she had to splash the soap off with one hand because Marnie had a death grip on her other arm…

As always, Pearl feels responsible for everything wrong with the family, every bloody dislocation. If she didn't have to go to school they could have stayed, avoiding the wrench of having to leave Aunty and Yanush behind in the only life she knew.

When she was little, Pearl liked waiting these tables that were higher than her head. It made her feel grown up and won her plenty of praise from the passers-through. Yanush and Red often got pissed while they were out pumping fuel. And so, Pearl would be sent to paint pictures in the caravan, away from the fight between her mum and dad that would surely follow. Beryl would try to distract Marnie by hollering for help in the kitchen. Unsettled, Pearl fell asleep amongst her finger paintings, not safe or far enough away because their yelling always woke her. In the morning, it was always the same, like nothing happened.

Pearl kicks off her runners and work clothes deciding that, come morning, she'll flat out ask Aunty what their plans are. What will they do when they sell and where will they go? She pulls on her white t-shirt nightie with a big strawberry on the front, thankful that she's not cleaning shitty bed pans at the hospital with her mad mum, yet. And 'Bubba' and 'Bear' are not miserably crammed into their ancient caravan in the next bay at the caravan park, yet.

Total fuckin' nightmare!

Chapter Four

Eddie admires the soft pink and blue hues of dawn as he eats a vegemite sandwich on the windmill platform. He squints over the dry desert plains at a tiny orange dust trail being kicked up by a trail bike fast approaching from about a kilometre inland. Behind it, he can just make out a tent pitched near the caves. Eddie drops a bit of crust for the cussing crow hopping about in the dirt below without once taking his eyes off the bike. Another crow swoops in to fight over it.

Pearl is awoken by the crows squabbling outside her room. She sits bolt upright and swings her legs out of bed, gasping, "Oh no, Curly!"

She races out of her room startling the noisy crows into flight. Eddie pulls back on the windmill platform so that Pearl won't see him. He watches her almost fall over Curly's empty jar, with a blue arrow painted on it, pointing toward the roadhouse.

Pearl's gaze follows the arrow to the grimy side window. She peers through it at Curly cruising in the huge fish tank that was full of dirt out the front yesterday. "Wo-ah," she breathes, wondering how it got up on a big old TV stand in the middle of the dining room and filled with water.

She runs around the front and into the roadhouse.

Eddie grins as he finishes his sandwich and returns to work oiling blade bolts.

Pearl circles the tank, drags over a red vinyl chair and climbs on it, twiddling her fingers on the surface to make Curly come up. "Hey Curly, amazing! Who put you in there?" She pulls a yellow post-it note off the side of the tank with her other hand and reads it: 'Windmill's pumping. Hope Curly likes his condo, Eddie.'

Pearl fancies she hears something under the steady buzz of the aerator, like faint splashing water and little kids giggling.

She leans closer to listen again, but the sound is obscured by the louder sound of a trail bike pulling in.

As soon as the bike sound stops, she hears the strange giggling again. Curly starts doing fast laps around the orange plastic fish lying dead on the bottom of the tank.

Pearl frowns and calls to him, "Whoa, chill, matey. I'll get it out."

She pushes her t-shirt sleeve over her shoulder and reaches for the sunken fish, but the tank is too deep and tall for her. She rises on her toes but is still too short, even on the chair. Pearl leans over the tank, takes a deep breath and pushes her face into the water.

Behind her, the trail bike rider enters. He rushes straight into the Gents toilet and shower room, wearing designer shades and a leather jacket over speedos, with bare legs and brown leather loafers, wallet and keys in hand. The toilet flushes, and he comes back out, halting at the sight of this tanned, leggy girl on her toes on a chair with her face in the fish tank. Her white knickers peek at him from out of the bottom of her t-shirt.

He pushes his shades on top of his head, mumbling, "Um ah."

Although only her face is in the water, Pearl feels herself diving fully into the tank.

What the…?

Astonishingly, Pearl feels her underwater-self doing big bird arms as if she's been swimming all her life. She surrenders to the feeling, heading down, t-shirt floating, bare feet frog kicking past the buzzing, bubbling aerator.

Down, down she swims, with Curly swimming alongside, goggling at her, his size small and in proportion with her on-land-self. Pearl smiles at him, because she's just imagining and it's a good feeling, amazing, until he darts past her to do more agitated laps around the dead plastic fish lying on the bottom of the tank.

Pearl's arms violently swing forward as she sees the front door of the roadhouse through the glass, but from outside,

32

where the tank used to be. The multi-coloured plastic strips blow about, looking bright and new and the glass of the front windows look sudsy and out of focus. Freaked out Curly darts for the surface, with his tail madly wagging, as Pearl takes this vision in like a dream that's fast turning into a nightmare. Her heart starts thumping and her lungs begin to burn.

A six-year-old girl appears beside the fish tank, wearing the mother-of-pearl necklace and a white, oversized cotton dress. She's bathing a naked two-year-old girl in the fish tank with Pearl, with a firm grip on her arm. Pearl reaches out to touch the toddler, but her hand passes straight through her. She snatches her hand back to her chest.

Euw! Gross!

The sounds she heard above the surface now make sense. The girl is humming to the happy toddler, who giggles as she squeezes bubbles out of the bum hole of the same orange plastic fish that Curly's freaked out about. Behind the girl, a woman is washing the windows of the roadhouse with a sudsy sponge, with her back to the children. The orange fish sinks, full of water. The toddler cries out in dismay, splashing water over the sides of the tank as she struggles to retrieve it, wriggling out of the older child's grip. The toddler's cry abruptly cuts off as she submerges.

"Mum!" the girl yells as she leans in to grab her back.

The soapy sponge drops from the mother's hand.

Spying the white necklace dangling in the water, the toddler latches on to it, tugging down hard, pulling the girl's face underwater too.

Pearl's eyes widen in fright, but she's relieved to see their mum racing in, dripping suds.

The toddler sees Pearl in the fish tank with her and gasps in horror, inhaling water. Pearl tries to save her, but again her hand goes through her and hits the glass.

The mother's hands surge in to drag both children out. She slaps the toddler's back to make her breathe. The toddler coughs out water and wails. The mother turns to the girl and wrenches the necklace over her head, deeply cutting her cheek on the shark tooth. The affronted six-year-old cries out in pain, holding her face, with blood on her fingers.

Pearl feels herself being pulled backwards, her vision disappearing violently like water down a plug hole.

Through the water, she hears a man calling to her, "Come out now!"

At the last moment, she grabs the sunken orange fish from the swirling bottom of the tank.

"*Signorina!*" the trail bike rider cries as he pulls Pearl's face out by a fist of t-shirt between her shoulder blades.

Pearl stares down at him from the height of the chair, chest heaving in breathless disbelief.

Beryl emerges from her bedroom rubbing her eyes and halts, confronted by this half-dressed man hanging on to her niece, who's standing on a chair over a fish tank that wasn't there when she went to bed!

"Get your hands off her!" she growls, making straight for the stranger.

He abruptly lets go of Pearl's t-shirt, extending the wet hand for Beryl to shake, saying, "*Scusa, signora.* I am Massimo. Massimo Venuti."

Pearl wipes her face with her t-shirt as her breathing slows. She looks at the plastic fish full of water in her hand and back into the tank, where Curly's marking time, gaping warily up at her.

Before she can make sense of what just happened, Beryl yells over her shoulder, "Bear!"

Alarmed, Massimo lowers his hand and exclaims, "Me, no, she, I am not a bear. I just came for milk and she, she."

Yanush charges out of the bedroom anticipating trouble, silencing frightened Massimo.

"Rented Land Cruiser with the two-fifty on the back," he informs Beryl. "Went through yesterday." He scowls at the fish tank and glares at Pearl, demanding to know, "Who filled that up? You?"

Pearl shakes her head. Beryl shrugs, not me. Yanush strides

to the side window, nodding to himself as he sees the windmill turning and Eddie working up on the platform.

He returns to Massimo and thrusts a paw out to shake, surprising him into taking a step back before reciprocating.

"Passing through?" Yanush asks.

"I am diving today in the caves, but not without breakfast, so I came for milk," Massimo explains. "Nobody was here so I used the *bagno*," he adds, casting a hand toward the Gents. "When I came out," he rushes, thrusting a palm up at Pearl, "*La... la signorina* had her head in the fish tank! So, I pulled her out."

Massimo is unnerved by their combined silence, adding, "What can I say?"

"*Italiano*, eh? I escaped from Estonia," Yanush reveals. "Milk's in the fridge," he adds, jutting his chin at the nearly empty drinks fridge pulled away from the dining room wall.

Relieved, Massimo dashes to the fridge and grabs a carton of milk.

Pearl climbs down from the chair to Beryl who, just like Marnie, hisses, "What'd you see in that water?"

Still in shock, Pearl stares at Beryl and back at the tank.

Beryl pins her with an unflinching look just like Marnie's, asking again, "Well?"

"I... I don't know. Little kids muckin' around at bath time... One nearly drowned."

Beryl stares stony eyed at the fish tank, not at Curly, who's cruising by looking chilled, now that the plastic fish is staying out. Pearl feels like she's crossed the line without knowing why. The last thing she wants is to rile Aunty.

"Must've been daydreaming or something," she mumbles, trying to breeze over it.

"Dreaming or drowning?" Beryl asks, glancing at Massimo for confirmation.

He shrugs, replying, "*Non lo so*," as he puts some coins on the counter beside the carton of milk.

Pearl stalks outside and chucks the plastic fish, muttering, "Why do I always have to do the talking?"

Massimo follows her out, eyeing Pearl appreciatively as she rounds his trail bike with two helmets in the crate on the back.

She glances back, notices his long, muscled legs and asks, "Do you usually ride like *that*?"

"*Scusa*," Massimo replies, hastily pulling his jacket together.

Yanush steps outside, followed by Beryl, who's carrying a glass of water, looking stressed.

As Massimo gets on his bike, Yanush asks him, "You from the north?"

"*Venezia, si.*"

"How many of you?"

"*Solo io.*"

Massimo sees Yanush looking at the other helmet in his crate as he pulls his out.

"We were two, but Cassandra and cave-diving don't mix," Massimo mutters, flicking the back of his hand up and out from under his chin, like good riddance, as he does up his helmet.

Yanush softens towards him, announcing, "A man can sleep alone, but he cannot eat alone. Come for dinner tonight."

"I can cook," surprised Massimo volunteers with a smile.

"Bravo!" Yanush replies, putting an arm around Beryl's shoulder to comfort her.

Massimo starts the bike, smiling broadly at Pearl, who calls out, "Don't forget your milk."

He looks inside, sees it on the counter and switches off the bike, muttering to himself, "*Stupido.*"

Pearl watches him heading back for the milk in his speedos, helmet and jacket with amusement. Two hunks in two days. Who says the Nullarbor's a desert?

She glances up and sees hunkalicious Eddie on the windmill platform and steps between his tools to look up at his back as he climbs down the ladder.

Beryl calls out, "Pearl. Come here!" but Pearl remains focused on Eddie, who's turning to face her at the base of the windmill, expecting appreciation.

Eddie's smile fades as he sees the intensity in Pearl's gaze.

He looks through the grimy side window at Curly, cruising in the giant tank, looking happy enough.

Beryl shrugs off Yanush's arm, calling again to Pearl, "Come here I said!"

"Why'd you do it?" Pearl asks Eddie.

"Nothing to it. Windmill's pumping. Just had to get the dirt out, fix the aerator and desalinate the water," he replies, unhappy with her tone. "A plain thank you would have been nice."

Pearl looks into Eddie's eyes and realises that he couldn't have seen what just happened from the windmill platform. He reads her gaze as renewed interest, which he instantly doubts because he hasn't got a clue how to read her. It doesn't stop him thinking about her *all the time.*

"Come up," he says, scooping up the oil refill bottle to avoid her strange scrutiny, "View's amazing."

As she follows Eddie up the windmill ladder, Massimo revs off on his trail bike with the carton of milk in his crate.

Eddie yells after him, "Forget your pants, looney?"

Pearl clambers on to the platform after Eddie and looks out, astonished to see the endless blur of blue on the horizon. She shakes her head, considering how she came all this way to get away from the ocean, only to find it lurking so close by. She scans her memories but cannot recall anyone ever taking her out there when she was little.

The events of the morning swirl in her head. How come she felt like she was swimming in the fish tank? And how come the girl bathing the toddler was wearing Great-Grandma's necklace? With the shark tooth in it.

Pearl shudders, remembering that Marnie has a little scar on her cheek, exactly where the shark tooth cut the six-year-old's face in her vision.

One thing's for sure: It all started when that 'thing' swam through her in the sea cave and that's still freaking Pearl out more than the shark.

Marnie's parting rant on her way to work echoes in her head, "Go on. Jump in the deep end and see what happens to ya. See if I care."

Pearl gazes at the blur of blue on the horizon wondering why Mum and Aunty are so tight-lipped. What are they hiding?

She has to find out – and maybe the answer's in the ocean. Even from this distance, Pearl feels its mysterious pull upon her.

Eddie's not looking at the sea. He's focused on Pearl, who returns his gaze, taking in the deep blue of his eyes, so like the ocean.

"Can you take me there?" she asks, pointing toward the cliffs.

"Where?" he replies, looking to where she's pointing. "That looney's tent?"

Pearl points past it to the cliffs, "No. There."

Eddie glances down at Beryl, finishing her water while urgently gesturing for Pearl to come down. He gives Pearl a conspiratorial nod. Her relieved gaze tells him that it's the perfect time to split.

Chapter Five

As Eddie approaches the cliffs in his ute, he glances at Pearl eagerly unbuckling her seat belt. She uncrosses her shapely thighs ready to leap out of the passenger seat the moment they stop. Pearl reaches for the door handle as he begins to pull up, well back from the cliffs.

Incredible!

It's just dirt and then nothing but never-ending sea. Pearl's glad that there's nobody about to notice that she's still in her long, strawberry t-shirt and bare feet. Worth it not to get grilled in her room by Aunty while trying to change.

"Better not stay long," Eddie rushes to say as she throws open the passenger door. "Beryl looked like she was having kittens."

"Raaah!" Pearl yells with a smirk, letting him know what she thinks of that as she jumps out of the ute and races for the cliffs. She leaves the passenger door wide open behind her, utterly energised by the salty smell of the ocean.

Eddie stares at Pearl through the windscreen. The wind rushes up from the edge, pulling her long t-shirt and wild hair back. The Southern Ocean roars, pounding the cliffs far below. Lethal. Afraid that she's either suicidal or reckless enough to slip and fall over the edge, Eddie sprints after Pearl with his heart thumping, leaving his door wide open, too.

Reminded of her last fierce leap, Pearl starts doing big bird arms as she runs faster for the edge, yelling, "*Haaaaaaa!*"

She looks ready to leap, but at the last moment pulls up, with both feet skidding in the gravel.

Too late for Eddie, who's launched into a footy tackle, slamming them both down to earth. Breathing hard, he rests his head between Pearl's shoulder blades, waiting for his heartbeat to slow. If this is how it feels to be high on adrenaline, he thinks, they should bottle it.

He breathes in her ear, "You're mad!"

"Reckon!" Pearl chuckles as she pushes back, rolling sideways to topple him off her.

But then he's beside her, wickedly gazing into her eyes as he rolls on his back, pulling her to sit astride him, with his hands on her hips.

Pearl feels Eddie hardening through his work shorts. Her thin white knickers become moist as he playfully pushes her hips forward and back a little. Her desire for him ignites and races south, just like it did on the bus.

Eddie pauses, his breath shortening, his eyes questioning: are you up for this?

Pearl is indecisive. If she lets him start kissing her again there'll be no turning back, which only makes her want him more.

But here? Now?

Her breath catches in her throat. Silence seems to expand all around her as she struggles to decide.

"Yeah?" Eddie dares to ask.

A pair of pink and grey galahs fly overhead, screeching, "*Naaaaah*," through the scorching sky.

Pearl exhales, climbs off Eddie and crawls to the edge, flattening out to look down at the waves smashing at the cliffs a hundred metres below. The rugged cliff face looks like a cream centred chocolate cake that a giant has taken huge bites out of. The soil beneath her seems to pulsate with life in such close proximity to sex and death. Pearl feels like her heart is pounding in time with the sea. Never before has she felt so on the edge of the world, so close to finding out something super important.

Besides what sex is like.

"No wonder they call it The Bight," she calls behind her to Eddie, but the sharp upward gusts of sea air snatch her words away.

Eddie commando crawls forward to look over the edge beside her with new eyes.

Pearl holds up a tiny, white seashell that she's scratched

out of the pebbly, ochre dirt. Eddie looks past the shell at her windswept features, exhilarated by the way she makes him do mad stuff, see things anew.

Pearl glances sideways at him, realising that she can't get rid of her desire for him that easily. There's a wild moment in her eyes as she leaps up, taking big steps backwards toward the ute, wondering what she wants with a boyfriend anyway.

"Let's go."

Eddie stares at her in disbelief.

Pearl smiles, infuriatingly reminding him, "Beryl. The kittens."

Eddie pushes himself up from a crouch, glances down at his bulging shorts and backs towards the ute like Pearl.

*

As soon as they arrive at the roadhouse, Beryl swipes the fly strips aside, calling,

"You two want breakfast?"

Eddie shakes his head, replying, "No thanks," as he heads up the windmill, "had a sandwich when I got up."

"I'll make my own," Pearl calls back to Beryl, "as soon as I get changed."

*

Pearl comes out of the kitchen eating a vegemite sandwich wearing a pair of shorts and one of her old painting shirts.

"Take the rest of those photos down," Yanush grumpily tells her, pointing his coffee mug at the section of the dining room not yet painted.

The landline rings in the office. He scowls as he goes to answer it, wondering what will happen if he hangs up on the debt collectors a second time today.

Pearl studies the old, framed photos as she takes them down. The largest features a younger, slimmer Beryl sitting beside well-built young Yanush. Their faces are illuminated by a campfire, way out the back of the rooms. Pearl scans the faces but doesn't recognise any of the locals or passers-through. In the dark behind the fire, she can just make out Red carrying wood toward the group. Marnie is beckoning her off the top of the wood heap where she's playing king of the castle with a couple of her pre-school blackfella mates.

Pearl strains to remember that night. She vaguely recalls having great fun playing with them, especially her little bestie, a boy called Youngy.

Beryl moves to gaze at the picture with Pearl, sighing nostalgically about the good old days, when they were solvent.

"Where'd everyone go?" Pearl asks. "Haven't seen a blackfella since I got back."

Beryl takes the picture off her and places it face down on one of the square dining tables, revealing a small sepia photo tucked under the frame.

"Some went to the sheep stations looking for work. The rest racked off to the cities years ago," Beryl answers.

"There's a big mob back at the caravan park, but Mum never let me hang with them," Pearl mutters.

"There's a reason for that," Beryl mutters, but Pearl ignores her; she's too engrossed in carefully sliding the old photo out of the back of the campfire picture and turning it over. They gaze at the sepia photo of a scrap of a teenage girl in front of the roadhouse, looking like she needs a reason to exist. She's wearing a tatty, white cotton dress and the family necklace with an old-fashioned suitcase beside her. It reminds Pearl of her vision in the tank of Marnie wearing the necklace when she was little, only this sad girl is older, and not her mum.

"Who's this?" she asks Beryl, touching the necklace in the photo, "Nana Raeleen?"

Beryl nods, reaching for it, "Was wondering where that went. I've hardly got any photos of Mum."

"How come she came here if she was born in Broome? And why isn't her dad, Peter Pearler, with her?" Pearl asks, frowning at the thought of her nana being abandoned out here with just a suitcase full of sadness. Even though it's a sepia photo, it's easy to see how dark Nana Raeleen was, but nobody in the family ever talks about that.

Beryl sighs heavily, plodding into her room to find Panadol and her eye-drops on the bedside table, confiding, "She was better off here, far from the mission and the ocean."

"Not that far, like bloody walking distance," Pearl calls after her, following Beryl in to nail her with a look, asking, "What is it with this family? Mum never let me in the ocean either."

"Didn't stop ya," Beryl snaps, furiously blinking out her eye drops as soon as they go in. "You should have known better than to jump off that cliff!" she adds, slamming down the bottle.

Pearl's gut clenches with anxiety. Was Aunty lying about Mum not calling, or maybe they talked while she was asleep?

"I saw you," Pearl hotly deflects. "In the fish tank."

"What?"

"You heard. And you saw me."

Beryl's buried that memory so deep that she's almost erased it. Her gaze looks wounded and her expression babyish as she remembers, with a jolt, seeing a scary girl in the tank with her way back then. She slumps to sit on the bed, burdened by the weight of remembering.

Pearl sits beside her, mesmerised.

Beryl swallows two Panadols with water. Triggered by these memories, she rubs her eyes hard. Her adult expression gradually returns as she wonders, Could the scary big girl in the tank have been Pearl? Who wasn't even *born*?

Beryl's tempted to tell Pearl everything so they can both try to understand. Yanush knows she sees things sometimes, but that's not the half of it, which is exactly how Beryl likes it. If Red could leave Marnie over it, then Beryl is never giving Yanush the same opportunity.

"Don't tell Yanush," she whispers. "Mum wouldn't let us have baths after that day when she was out washing the windows, and we...."

"Nearly drowned," Pearl says for Beryl, who doesn't need reminding now that she's remembered.

"Suited us," Beryl shrugs, suspiciously eyeing the water in the bedside glass. "We even had to have our eyes closed in the shower."

"Ye-ah, me, too," Pearl replies.

Beryl turns to look in Pearl's eyes as she asks, "Why'd you stick your head in that fish tank?"

"Just wanted to get the plastic fish off the bottom," Pearl answers, "Curly didn't like it. Lucky Nana Raeleen pulled you two out, eh?"

Beryl nods. Her vision clouds and thumping head are telling her loud and clear that she can't handle this. Besides, some secrets can't be safely deposited in an eighteen-year-old's head. Safer to say nothing, like she agreed on the phone with Marnie.

Pearl rubs the space between her breasts, needing to tell someone about the thing that swam through her. She can see that Aunty's struggling, but someone has to talk some time.

"Is it because we're Aboriginal?" she asks.

Beryl looks at Pearl like she just threw a pie in her face.

"Come on, Aunty. They don't put white kids in missions. Maybe we're watered down, but we've got all year tans, skinny legs and big noses," Pearl jokes, trying to make light of something she needs confirmed right now.

"Stop stirring things up," Beryl chips her for even asking.

Here we go.

Beryl presses her thumbs into her temples to try to ease the throbbing.

"Thought you'd be different," Pearl mutters as she stands, ready to head back to work in the dining room. "But you're not. You're just as tight-lipped and superstitious as Mum."

Beryl gets up and lunges for Pearl, pulling her into a fierce hug that there's no getting out of.

"Nana Pearl's spirit in the ocean, luv," Beryl blurts out before she can stop herself. "And that's all I'm gunna say about it."

Pearl gapes.

"Pearl!" Yanush calls through. "These pictures won't take themselves down."

Pearl walks into the dining room feeling queasy. Could Great-Grandma Pearl's spirit have swum through her… to scare off the shark?

Maybe she was trying to protect me?

Maybe she made the fish swim in a ball to hide me?

That's fucking insane!

One thing's for sure: once Aunty clams up there's no un-clamming her…

Pearl gazes sideways at the fish tank. Well, asking questions isn't the only way to find things out.

*

Pearl is patching the last wall as Massimo walks in wearing a black chef's apron over jeans and a clean white shirt, carrying his mobile phone, charger and a small speaker.

"*Buongiorno, signorina,*" he greets her, holding up the phone. "Could I charge this please?"

Pearl's concerned expression changes into something resembling a smile.

Massimo is dazzled by his first glimpse of her very pink tongue and that cute little crease above her top lip, which disappears as Pearl says, "No use charging it. Mobiles don't work out here."

Massimo nods, "*Si,* but it has music."

Yanush walks in from the kitchen in time to notice the flirtatious look in Massimo's eyes.

"*Buongiorno, signor chef,*" he says, slapping Massimo on the back as he steers him into the kitchen.

"Enter *la cucina.* You like wodka? I like wodka."

*

Pearl is finishing the patching as Massimo reappears to retrieve his partially charged phone. He puts on an Italian pop song and plugs in the speaker, while scrolling through to show Pearl his cave photos as proudly as a mother offering baby snaps.

45

"You have seen them, these caves?"

Pearl shakes her head, wondering what else they've kept from her.

"They're phenomenal, forgotten places."

Pearl takes a closer look, intrigued by the eerie torch-lit walls and ice-blue, mysterious cave water beyond. Something white like crystal seems to sparkle beneath the rocky ledges.

"Didn't say I wouldn't go," she replies, looking hopefully up at him.

Massimo smiles like he has no plan to stop smiling any time soon. A delicious warm feeling is spreading though him because this *bellissima* is interested in the caves, unlike Cassandra.

"What's he singing about?" Pearl asks about the pop song, surprised to hear the English words, 'singing in the rain', in the Italian tune.

Massimo moves close to confide, "Nirvana lessons for selfie addicts. We chant mantras we don't understand. *Nam-aste*," he sings along, putting his hands together, bowing to her in a parody of prayer. "That's our karma, according to Gabbani's pop philosophy."

Pearl has no idea what he's on about, but she could listen to his deep, accented voice all day. She likes his black curly hair and how quickly his dark, almost black eyes turn cheeky. He's classical, a pure bred, she decides, like the roman statues they studied in history. Not a bitsa like her – Broome creole, whatever that means. Pearl eyes the curve of Massimo's hooked nose above his perfect cupid lips, wondering what they'd be like to kiss. What if he leaned forward right now? He'd have to, 'cause he's so tall. She stares at his broad swimmer's chest right before her eyes.

To die for.

Yanush calls through the servery, "Mass-imo, your onions are burning."

"*Scusa*," Massimo says, rushing back.

"Ha! Gotcha. Have some more wodka," Yanush chuckles, topping up Massimo's glass as soon as he enters the kitchen.

"*Nostarovia!*"

Through the servery he sees the framed photos leaning against the wall and calls through, "Put them in the caravan, please, Pearl, in case they get paint on them."

Still headachy, Beryl emerges from the bedroom and slumps on to a dining chair, peering into the kitchen at her big Bear cooking with Massimo, who's taller, but only half Bear's width. Yanush shoves a huge spoonful of sauce into his mouth, humming with pleasure.

"I will make more," Massimo says, sloshing milk into the pot.

Yanush adds another huge splash of vodka.

Massimo gapes at him, saying, "But this dish requires brandy."

Yanush 'tastes' another huge spoonful. "*Perfecto*," he announces, licking his lips. "In Estonia, we say a man who does not know how to cook, does not know how to love."

Massimo frowns. "Cassandra said the only person that I will ever love is me."

"Not a bad place to start," Yanush replies.

Massimo pensively applies himself to cutting up what is left of the dried herbs, adding, "My mother says it only happens once in a lifetime. The right one will only come out when I forget where to look, which is, of course, ridiculous."

He peeks at Pearl, heading out to the caravan carrying framed photos.

"You have to be lucky," Yanush responds. "If Bubba's water tower hadn't fallen over, I would never have fallen for her."

Beryl calls through to the kitchen, "Bloody lucky, meeting a sexy Olympic weight-lifter way out here. Million to one. Right when I needed him, too."

"Olympian, eh?" Massimo asks, glancing at Yanush's big belly.

Yanush sticks it out further, saying, "Lucky I got away when I jumped ship. Better than starving in Siberia if they caught me."

"I don't believe in luck," Massimo says.

"Fate?"

Massimo shakes his head disdainfully.

"*Niente*. No prophecies from the gypsies about Cassandra being the one either."

"When the right one comes, you will know," Yanush replies, padding out to lovingly massage Beryl's temples, asking Massimo, "How old are you anyway, mid-twenties?"

"Twenty-seven."

"Plenty of time to find her," Yanush assures him. "But your heart needs to be broken a few times first."

He gives Beryl a kiss on the top of her head, saying, "Love takes practice. Lots of practice."

Massimo nods, unconvinced that he'll ever experience such a love.

Pearl walks back in and feeds Curly fish flakes. Through the tank, she notices how loyal and loving 'Bear' is with his 'Bubba'. It makes her wish that she had a dad like that, or a boyfriend like that, if she could ever trust one not to hurt or leave her.

She pensively wipes her fingerprints off the sides of the tank with a tea towel as Curly pecks at the flakes. Pearl frowns remembering baby Beryl's terrified face inhaling water at the sight of her in there with her. Way too scary.

No wonder they think seeing stuff's a curse that's been passed down. Are Mum and Aunty just trying to protect me? From what?

If Great-Grandma Pearl was cursed, how come she passed it down to the lot of us?

And who the hell cursed her?

Chapter Six

Beryl and Pearl are seated opposite each other on two pushed-together dining tables, with Yanush at the end and Eddie beside Beryl.

Massimo showily carries in a serving dish of flaming hamburger patties soaked in Yanush's vodka, impressing everyone except Eddie. Massimo places the dish before Pearl with a flourish. The flames extinguish as he sits beside her, opposite Eddie.

"Steak *au-poivre* with a little *fantasia*," he announces. "The beef patties are fillet, and the vodka is brandy."

"What's wrong with spag bol?" Eddie asks.

Massimo looks across the table at him with disdain, "Bolognese requires fresh tomato sauce, fresh *basilico* and fresh pasta."

"Tastes good to me," Pearl reckons, piling her fork with a second serve of saucy beef patty.

"Yeah, lovely tucker," Beryl agrees with her mouth full.

Yanush tops up his vodka, stands and proposes a toast to Massimo, "Here's to us and those who love us, and bugger those who don't!"

Massimo stands and raises his glass, "*Salute!*"

Yanush sits, quietly filling in Beryl, "His girlfriend buggered off."

"Wonder why?" Eddie asks, overhearing.

Pearl's amused by the adversarial looks Eddie and Massimo are shooting across the table at each other, like bullets.

"How long you here for?" Beryl asks Massimo. "We've got rooms out the back going cheap."

Massimo shrugs, not about to confide in these strangers about his 'pilgrimage' to find himself in forgotten places.

"I'm not sure," he replies, "but I love to dive in this cave," he adds, finding Beryl a photo in his phone. "It's amazing."

"Alone?" Eddie asks.

"Obviously."

"Not a good idea."

"Why not?" Massimo asks, spreading his hands. "The water is as clear as air and the walls curve so sensuously, like the contours of a woman's… but what would you know?"

"Tell you what I know, *mate*," Eddie snaps. "A diver died down there a while back. Stirred up the silt and couldn't find his way back. So get yourself a buddy who knows the terrain."

"I will take Pearl," Massimo smugly shoots back.

"No you don't," Beryl snaps, pushing Massimo's phone aside. "Blackfellas reckon there's a spirit in that water."

Pearl gives Beryl an indomitable look usually reserved for Marnie.

"I'm eighteen, Aunty. Do what I like."

"If Bubba says you're not, you're not," Yanush growls. "You're here to work."

Pearl glares at Yanush, who suddenly looks less like a nice, big performing bear and more like a fat rat with a pointy nose, ice blue eyes and pursed lips.

"No *problema*," Massimo says, like all has been amicably decided, "We will go before work."

Pearl gives him a tiny, excited nod, which is not lost on Eddie, who pulls the ring top off his second can of bourbon and cola with a sharp snap.

"You go too," Yanush tells him.

Eddie nods.

"These… how you say, First Nation's people, where can I find them?" Massimo asks, looking from Pearl to Beryl.

Look no further!

"They all buggered off years ago," Beryl replies, avoiding his gaze.

"So," Massimo muses, "It's an ancient water spirit. *Interessante*."

"And that poor diver," Beryl adds.

"Do the ancient ones believe that your spirit is trapped in the water if you drown?" Massimo asks.

Eddie's stare hardens at being reminded of his mother's drowning.

"Dunno," Beryl responds with her face closing shop just like Marnie's.

Yes you do.

"I know!" Pearl pipes up, glaring at Beryl, who glares back.

"What?"

"Don't go anywhere near that water," Beryl warns, "and throw some cave dirt in to hide him from the spirit before he dives in. Right?"

"Right."

*

Eddie lies in bed trying to get his mind off the wild sex he wanted to have with Pearl on the cliffs. He starts reading an article in *The Countryman* about rods for windmills, but soon throws it aside. He irritably rubs the gold nugget at his clavicle back and forth on its strap, wondering where he stands with Pearl, who both attracts and repels him with her crazy shit. Why he's attracted to a mad woman like his mother who might drown at any moment is beyond him. He just fixes windmills, and Pearl's going whichever way the wind blows, he reminds himself. He'd rather focus on what trouble this pumped up, reckless wog is going to cause him, and Pearl.

Outside, the wind's howling, making the windmill clank, keeping him awake; and then he hears it, Yanush's drunken singing, interrupted by straining sounds.

*

Yanush is under the white caravan, lifting the chassis like Olympic weights, singing, "Once in a lifetime every star in the sky shines for one reason, to light your way to the one love you'll find, once in a lifetime."

51

Amused, Massimo stands nearby holding his bike helmet, watching the round white caravan going up and down in the moonlight in time with each straining grunt. The empty vodka bottle lies discarded near Yanush's big, hairy legs in boots sticking out from under the van.

"*Bravo*, Yanush!" Massimo calls under the van. "It is true. You are strong like a bear."

"Still got it, Bubba," Yanush yells at the roadhouse.

"But a singer you are not," Massimo adds, as he straightens to put on his helmet.

Beryl comes out of the roadhouse in a white nightie with a torch, which she shines under the van.

"Come on, Bear," she calls to him, "Time to go to sleep."

"Thank you for your hospitality, *signora*," Massimo says, peering under the van again. "I hope I will not find you here in the morning, *signor*."

Massimo mounts and guns the bike, flicks the headlights on and weaves a little as he rides the trail to his tent, narrowly missing a Bob-tailed lizard creeping across the access road.

As he dismounts, Massimo spies an ancient shell glinting white, stuck in the tyre of his four-wheel drive. He plucks it out and rubs it between his thumb and forefinger, wondering what mysteries about the meaning of his life will be answered with gorgeous *Perla*, diving in the haunted cave under the desert in the morning. Whatever this trip is turning out to be, he's happy that it's not mediocre.

*

Thoughts of things seen in the fish tank are keeping Pearl as much from sleep as the high wind and clanking windmill. She's thankful that Yanush has finally stopped singing. She sits at the bedside table painting a splodge of orange fish on the bottom of a watery blue wash on paper curling at the edges from being in her rucksack. Pearl swishes her brush in the cloudy water in Curly's jar and peers into the painting. She leans forward, closes her eyes to remember, opens them and starts painting exactly what she saw.

*

There's shock on six-year-old Marnie's face, and Beryl, the-two-year-old's, who's yanking hard on the gleaming white necklace around Marnie's neck, holding her under. Terrified baby Beryl's big brown eyes stare directly out of the painting at Pearl-the-painter, whose hand is painted going straight through baby Beryl in the tank.

Pearl's hands shake as she puts the paintbrush down. She can't escape the feeling that she traumatised baby Beryl when all she was trying to do was save her.

Is that why they think seeing's a curse? Because it terrifies everybody?

Deeper inside that feeling, past secrets, guilt and family shame, Pearl senses something of primal importance. There must be a reason why her bloodline can 'see' in water. Pearl silently commits to not giving up, no matter what they say, even if it kills her. No way is she giving up until she finds out exactly what that reason is.

She fingers the shell pieces in the heirloom necklace like rosary beads, wondering how she is going to solve this mystery with two hotties hanging around.

*

Eddie is startled awake by the sound of Massimo's trail bike starting up. He checks his watch – six-thirty – and races to open the door, but it's too late. The bike is already revving up the trail toward Massimo's tent and the caves.

Ochre dust billows behind helmeted Pearl in a bright floral dress, clinging to bare-legged Massimo in his leather jacket.

"Safety gear!" Eddie yells as he rushes 'round the front to retrieve his ute keys from the servery counter.

He almost smacks straight into Yanush standing in a flurry of plastic strips in the doorway wearing white boxer shorts, saluting him with a glass of bubbling Berocca.

"Got a lot to learn, kid," Yanush tells him.

He downs the orange hangover cure in one gulp.

Beryl pushes past Yanush in her white nightie, rounds the building and stops abruptly in Pearl's open doorway.

She sees the painting on Pearl's bed and yells, "Bear! Come quick."

*

Beryl and Yanush sit side by side on Pearl's bed looking at her painting in Beryl's shaking hands. Terrified baby Beryl is staring out at them with Pearl's hand passing through her.

Beryl blurts out, forgetting that she had decided against confiding in Yanush, "That's exactly how I felt, seeing a spirit in there with me and Marnie. Mum thought it was her mum, Nana Pearl, but it was … our Pearl, 'cause she saw me… yesterday… How is that even possible, Bear?"

Yanush pensively scratches the stubble on his chin, suggesting, "Maybe you see the future and Pearl sees the past?"

Beryl nods, considering this. She hands him the painting and holds her head groaning, "We've got to protect her."

Yanush puts the painting on the bedside table.

"She's not six anymore, Bubba."

"Doesn't matter. Get down there. Get her back."

Yanush tilts Beryl's face up to look into her eyes, "If she sees, she sees. There's no sharks in there. Eddie will be on his way soon."

Beryl puts her trembling hands inside his, "Feels bad, Bear."

"Too much worry, Bubba."

*

Massimo sits on a mound of lumpy limestone rocks to pull his air tanks on over his wet suit and buoyancy compensator.

Pearl aims his head torch over the glinting water to the far wall of the cave. She's enthralled and excited to see hand paintings there. The ancients blew the ochre paint out of their mouths at their hands, she learned at school. To reach them, she

54

must wade into the shallow water in the eerily humid air of the cave.

The limestone walls look smooth, nearly white, and the water has a blue-white shimmer.

Pearl hesitates, scoops up some limestone dirt and scatters it into the clear cave water to hide Massimo from the spirit, like Beryl told her to. She shudders as she watches it clouding the pristine visibility. She tucks her dress into her knickers and wades in up to her calves, edging around the top to reach the back wall. There, Pearl leans forward to press her hands on top of the painted hands, with the family necklace glinting luminously at her throat.

Massimo looks on, captivated. He silently slides into the deepest section in water as clear as air so that he appears to be suspended in space.

Pearl doesn't notice him. She is too absorbed in the eerie beauty of this ancient water hole beneath the arid desert above. Is this Eddie's 'giant underground sea'?

Massimo pulls his mask on, pushes the regulator into his mouth and slides beneath the surface, approaching in a halo of bubbles, without once taking his gaze off Pearl's feet in the water. He surfaces, eyeing her luscious long legs and dress tucked into her white knickers.

He pulls the regulator out and his mask back on to his head, calling, "Come in, *Perla*. It's amazing."

Pearl turns, leaning close to the wall, mumbling, "Nah, nah, too cold."

Massimo rises fast, grabs her waist and laughs as he falls back into the water holding her.

Shocked, Pearl kicks to hold herself up, pleading, "No, n-not my head under, not in here."

"Don't be afraid," Massimo soothes, gazing into Pearl's fearful eyes, and kisses her.

Before Pearl can react, he glides them further back into deep section and slides off her head torch. Pearl pulls out of the kiss as the water rises over their faces.

Her eyes widen underwater as she sees a wisp of a brown girl painting something over the ancient hands on the cave wall, in the shadowy light of a flickering flame at her feet. Her simple brush strokes soon reveal a girl jumping off a cliff, descending fast, feet first with flailing arms.

Is that… me?

Pearl urgently kicks off Massimo and bird-frogs forward to better see this vision. At the edge of the wall, she shuffles her hands upwards to stay under, peering up through the surface at the young, half-dressed painter.

Massimo doesn't know what she is doing but knows better than to disturb her.

The water near Pearl suddenly comes alive with movement as the other tribal women wade over in a flurry of brown feet. They climb on to the ledge to mill around the painter. Some drop their water baskets as they stare at her work, nervously whispering and glancing behind them like she's going to be in big trouble. The painter crosses her arms, sure of what she has painted. She flings a hand at the cave water, indicating that's where she saw this vision and why she painted it.

A deep, angry male voice echoes across the cave from the entrance, startling the tribal women into intense, irate whispering in a language that Pearl can't understand. The women mill together in the shallow water, nudging each other indignantly as they glare at the furious elder with horizontal scars across his chest, storming toward them. He stomps through the shallows very close to Pearl with broad brown feet.

The incensed tribe's women jeer and scatter before him. They scoop up their water baskets fast, sloshing water over the sides, as they scramble out of the rocky entrance of the cave.

The young painter is left alone at the wall, defiantly unwilling to face the elder. Instead, she looks down at her feet and further down into the water.

Pearl's eyes widen with astonishment as they recognise each other through the eerie veil of time. The thing, with the terrible see-through smile that swam through Pearl in the sea cave, now stands above her, alive, well and absolutely Aboriginal.

Pearl struggles, dangerously short of air, but she cannot surface and leave her ancestor with this angry man.

Her gut clenches as the elder yanks the painter's shoulder back to make her face him. He wrenches her away from the wall, revealing Pearl diving off a cliff, painted over the ancient hand paintings. He glares at her work, believing that she has painted what she intends to do. He spits on the painting and splashes cave water over it to erase it, yelling as he rubs it off.

This time, she's gone too far, he thinks, painting over the hands of their ancestors without permission. She must be taught a lesson, but he will not sing her to her death. He is as angry as scared for her. If she jumps off the nearby cliffs, she will die.

In a split second, he knows what he must do to both stop her threatening the authority of her elders and to save her before she goes too far. If she believes a shark will take her, she will not jump. What she needs is some time alone in the desert to think about what she has done. She needs to go walk-a-bout and come back knowing her place. He stands over her with eyebrows pushed together above his intensely focused glare as he withdraws a shark tooth from his totem collection in a straw bag at his waist. He throws it at Pearl's ancestor with the severest of banishment gestures. The shark tooth lands in her water basket.

Bastard!

"*Marbun?*" Pearl's ancestor asks, quavering with fear as she looks down at the shark tooth.

He does not deny it. Her head hangs with shame and grief as she accepts her fate, sloshing right past Pearl and trudging toward the rocky cave opening carrying her water basket.

Pearl fingers the shark tooth at her throat as she kicks up and surfaces, violently breaking the vision. She sobs in air, stands and then doubles over, furious and overawed for a chest-heaving moment, to try to process the injustice of what she has just witnessed.

Massimo wades forward and kneels, looking up into Pearl's teary eyes, confused and concerned.

Still breathless, she pushes him aside, turns, squats and ducks her head under again to try to see if she can glimpse her ancestor's flight from the cave, but the vision is broken.

Pearl longs for this connection between herself and her cursed, First Nation's great-grandma to stay open, like it's the most important thing in her life, but her ancestor is long gone, long dead.

Massimo tilts her chin out of the water, commanding, "Breathe."

Pearl wrenches free to duck under again and double checks if it really was herself jumping off the cliff in that painting, but the moment has passed. Only the ancient hand paintings remain.

Massimo takes her by the shoulders and lifts her head and torso out of the water.

"Let me go," Pearl growls, from somewhere angry and breathless in the back of her throat.

She wrenches out of Massimo's grip in an adrenaline rush and scrambles over the rocks toward the cave's entrance.

Massimo calls after her, "Wait, please, *Perla! Madonna mia!* What is the matter with you?"

Pearl can't wait. She rushes out of the cave as fast as the incensed tribe's women did before her.

Massimo wrenches off his fins, tanks and buoyancy compensator, furious at himself.

"I'm sorry," he calls after her. "*Stupido!*" he curses as he throws his tanks on to the ledge in the bobbing light of the discarded head torch.

Dripping wet, Pearl sprints into the stark sunlight, past surprised Eddie, who reels back from peeking in Massimo's tent. Pearl doesn't see him, or his ute parked behind the tent. She races straight to Massimo's trail bike, relieved to find the keys in it, guns it and revs off, heading fast for the roadhouse in a cloud of dust.

Eddie calls after her, "Pearl! Wait! What happened?"

He turns and sees Massimo hobbling over the rocks at the cave's entrance, barefoot in his unzipped wetsuit.

"What did you do to her?" Eddie yells, striding over to confront Massimo.

"I kissed her," Massimo dryly responds. "She left. Never happened to me before."

The men glare at each other and then both hear the unmistakable sound of a shotgun being snapped together. They turn and see Norm, the burly station owner, steadily approaching with his gun levelled at Massimo, who throws his hands up.

Norm looks well and truly capable of murder with a couple of dead rabbits slung over his blue-singleted shoulders, dripping blood on his beer gut, shorts and work boots.

"Who's this?" he asks Eddie, jutting his chin at Massimo.

"Wog cave diver."

Norm steps back, still pointing the shotgun at Massimo as he peers in the window of Massimo's flash four-wheel drive, demanding, "Give us ya keys."

"Do as he says," Eddie warns. "You're on his land."

Massimo looks around, spreading his hands in the air, spluttering, "There is no fence. I did not know."

He leans into his tent, startling a Thorny Devil Lizard, who hightails it into the corner as Massimo backs out, throws Norm the keys and raises his hands again.

Norm chucks the rabbits in the back seat of the four-wheel drive and orders Massimo, "Get in. You," he tells Eddie, "in the front."

Massimo gingerly nudges the bloody rabbits aside with his wet-suited bum as he gets in the back of his hire car with his hands still up.

Chapter Seven

Yanush looks up from leaning over to pour paint into a roller tray as Pearl roars up to the roadhouse on Massimo's trail bike with both helmets in the crate. He puts the tin down as she kicks the stand down, gets off the bike and marches toward her room like a wet, wound-up stick insect.

"Bubba's been worried sick," he yells out of the front door after her. "Where's Eddie?"

"Dunno," Pearl yells back, glancing up the windmill. "Why?"

Hung over, Yanush irritably rubs the sweat off his forehead with his headband. The paint fumes are turning his gut. He pads outside for fresh air.

"There in a tick," Pearl yells from her room. "Just gotta change."

"So much for her not going in!" Beryl rants as she rushes past Yanush and into Pearl's room, demanding to know, "You alright? What happened?"

Pearl stands before her, dripping wet.

"Great-Grandma Pearl was Aboriginal," she tells Beryl, point blank.

"Nah," Beryl responds, averting her gaze. "We're Irish from Peter Pearler, with a bit of Broome Creole mixed in. You know that."

Pearl pulls off her wet dress and yanks an oversized, paint-splodged shirt over her head.

She changes into a dry bra and knickers under it, insisting, "The Pearler might have come from Ireland, but Great-Grandma was from a tribe right here, until one of the men sent her packing."

"You saw Nana Pearl's spirit? In the cave?"

Pearl nods, asking, "What's *marbun*?"

"Curse," Beryl replies with a sharp intake of breath. "Who

said that?"

Through the window, they see Yanush, stomping toward them with a paint brush in his hand.

Pearl rushes to reply, "She did. She was an artist too. And she saw me!"

Beryl sits on Pearl's bed, tensely rubbing her eyes.

"Enough mumbo jumbo," Yanush snaps, thrusting the paintbrush at Pearl. "Get to work."

Pearl stomps 'round the front, dips her brush in the paint tray and starts filling in the edges around the front door. She pulls the rustling plastic strips aside, straining to hear what cranky Yanush is saying to Aunty about her in her room.

"I don't want to hear it, Bubba," he argues. "Every day something: food, water, men, hocus pocus. And every day what about you? Headaches, eye aches. Anymore, and she goes!"

"We're not sending her back, Bear," Beryl insists. "Maybe she's come to break the curse?"

"If she doesn't kill you first!" Yanush roars.

Pearl's heard enough. She marches 'round to her room and confronts them.

"I'm not gunna kill anyone!" he roars back at Yanush, "So you can stop talking about me like that," she adds, hurt. "I'm only here 'cause I love Aunty. And you, ya old crank!"

Yanush pulls a pair of scissors out of his back pocket and slaps them on Pearl's painting.

"See Bubba's toenails?" he asks. "You know who cuts them? I do. Why? Because she can't see her own toenails anymore. You want to help around here, or be a good-for-nothing artist?"

"Help," Pearl mulishly mutters.

"Then shut up and cut Bubba's toenails," Yanush snaps as he heads back to the dining room.

Pearl glances at Beryl, who gives her a cheeky look and kicks off her thongs.

She swings a leg up on the bed, saying, "Go on then."

Pearl sets to work, but the corner of her aunty's big toenail is a bit dug in. She tries to pry it up with the edge of the scissors.

"Ow! Watch it!"

"Sorry, Aunty."

Beryl tsks and puts her foot back on the floor, saying, "Bit of a shock, finding out like that, eh? Told you not to go in that cave water."

"You could have told me," Pearl mutters, thinking so unfair, always being the last to know.

"Could never get much out of Mum," Beryl responds. "Didn't know for sure until you told me!"

"We're brown," Pearl states. "I just don't feel Indigenous, whatever that's supposed to feel like. If Mum knew, she never said either."

Pearl starts to pace, muttering, "Wish Mum hadn't called me Pearl."

"Maybe Nana Pearl's spirit's restless," Beryl muses. "She got kicked out, you say? Mum always said Nana's mob weren't friendly."

Pearl confirms it, "Yeah. Some old bastard didn't like her painting… me."

Beryl squints.

"What?" she asks, pulling Pearl's arm to sit beside her again because all her pacing is making Beryl giddy.

Yanush returns, peering at the women through the window, sitting side by side, conspiratorially sharing secrets. Pearl and Beryl see him coming and go quiet.

"Enough," he snaps from the doorway. "I want that wall finished today."

He looks at Pearl and casts a hand toward the roadhouse, following her back in to help.

*

Norm savagely crunches the gears of Massimo's hire car as he drives up a beaten track like a madman. He eyes Massimo in the rear-view mirror, still holding his hands up.

Massimo can't see much of him, except his steely blue-grey eyes and puffy, red drinker's nose.

"Can't see," Norm says. "Put ya hands down."

Massimo snaps on his seat belt, recoiling from the rabbits leaking blood beside him.

Norm squints with amusement and pushes back his Akubra, adding, "And don't try anything with those rabbits."

Eddie grins.

Massimo sees that he's been had.

To make matters worse, Norm starts raucously singing as he guns it up the driveway of his run-down station, "*Arseolo mio*, la, la, la, la," making Eddie laugh.

Alarmed, Massimo stares through the windscreen at a dilapidated old crop duster, fast descending on a collision course. Close to impact, he crosses his arms in front of his face and braces against the back of Eddie's seat.

At the last moment, Norm bumps the four-wheel drive off the broad track.

The pilot, wearing old-fashioned flying goggles, safely lands the crop duster, pulling it to a rattling halt alongside.

As the trio get out of the car, the short pilot jumps down from the crop duster looking like a jockey beside tall Massimo, who only has eyes for the mountain of rusting junk strewn all over the place. Norm has collected many old cars, kerosene fridges, plate glass, broken bits of engines and bald tyres over the years.

Massimo's broad chest, sweaty in his unzipped wetsuit, is at eye level with the pilot who is looking him up and down like he's the statue of David.

He turns to ask Norm, "Who's *this*?"

"Trespasser."

"Massimo Venuti," Massimo says, wiping the rabbit blood down the front of his wet suit, ready to shake.

The pilot ignores his bloodied hand.

"I'm Ray the Postie," he grins, revealing a wide gap between his two front teeth. "I see you've met Norm."

Norm notices Massimo looking around again and asks, "Like the place?"

"Words can't describe it," Massimo dryly replies, lowering his hand.

"We're turning it into a tourist ranch," Norm begins and Ray joins in, "called County Downs."

"I'm sure many Italians will flock here," Massimo responds, glancing at the ignition to see if Norm has left his keys in it, "if word gets out."

Norm smiles, asking Ray, "What did I tell ya?"

Ray puffs out his chest and removes his flying goggles and leather cap, revealing his shiny, bald head.

Massimo is relieved to have prompted their change of mood.

"I can cook *coniglio*," he says, jutting his chin at the dead rabbits.

"Bewdy," Norm replies, turning to Ray. "Get him a beer."

Ray gambols over junk in the front paddock to get to one of the kerosene fridges, sending Norm's Brahman bull, Bonox, off at a trot. He staggers back with a carton of Victoria Bitter.

Eddie smiles, certain they'll be there all night.

Massimo glances at grinning Norm and relaxes for the first time since being held at gunpoint by this madman.

*

Pearl stays up late emptying the contents of her head on to a painting. She paints herself as a dark brown girl of twelve, being held back from chasing after her white dad, Big Red, as he roars off for good in his beat-up ute. Her younger, slimmer mum, Marnie, also painted dark, is holding her back, like a scowling anchor on the end of her arm.

Young Pearl's mouth is painted wide open.

Her pink tongue commands all the attention in the painting that she failed to receive as a kid, wailing, "*Waaaaaaaaiit!*"

Beryl shuffles through the open door in her nightie, muttering, "Bear's snoring his head off."

She sees Pearl's dark, anguished face in the painting and puts an arm around her.

"Is that us now, blackfellas?"

Pearl confronts her aunty, demanding to know, "Well aren´t we? There's family out there we've never even *met*!"

Beryl shakes her head, replying, "There's none around here anymore, I told ya. It's messy. Nana Pearl got kicked out and cursed like you said. After she died, Mum got too jinxed by her dad, Peter Pearler, to make contact with Nana's mob, even though he brought her back here to Nana's country. She wanted to make contact, but Dad always told her: what good's it gunna do ya trying to find family who don't want ya? Not that he'd have been too excited about losing her back to the mob, mind you, so he didn't lift a finger to help her."

Pearl scowls, unhappily reminded of Marnie saying: "Why glorify a prick who doesn't even want to know ya?"

She squints at her traumatised, darker-self racing after Red's ute in her painting, not relishing the thought of further rejection, but Aunty's sounding like rejection works both ways.

She stares at Beryl and asks, "*Who* doesn't want to know *who*?"

Beryl deflects to the painting, saying, "It's not why Red took off, Luv. Was probably just Marnie, driving him up the wall like she drives everyone up the wall."

"He could have taken me with him," Pearl mutters.

"It's no life for a young girl out prospecting, Luv."

Try as she might to console Pearl's heartache, it just makes Beryl reflect on her own father, all of their fathers, for that matter...

"Peter Pearler took Mum to a mission when Nana Pearl died, 'cause he already had a white wife and kids," she reveals, shocking Pearl, who's never heard that before. "When he found out that the mission was using her up, making her slave for nuthin', he got work for her out here in Nana's Pearl's country, 'cause that's where she wanted to live. At least she got paid by old Ron, who married her after his wife died. He fathered us kids and willed her this place."

"Was Grandad Ron white?" Pearl asks, since nobody ever says.

Beryl nods, revealing, "He was good to Marnie and me, Mum always said, but he died when we were little, so we hardly knew him. Dads. Duds the lot of 'em. Red wasn't the only one. They all either died or left us for dead."

Pearl feels churned up, wondering what's the use of dads if there're none worth having.

"So not fair," she mumbles. "If Nana Raeleen went to a mission, she was black."

"Light chocolate, just the way they liked 'em," Beryl confirms. "Too brown for white; too white for black, she used to say. And no, it's not fair. At least you'll always have your mum and me. Yanush too. He may get cranky, when he thinks I need protecting, but he loves you."

"Is Mum still pissed off that I left?" Pearl asks.

Beryl raises her eyes.

"She'll simmer down. Give it time."

Pearl nods, looking Beryl in the eye, "Are you *sure* you never heard from Dad? All this time? He never passed through?"

"God's honour," Beryl answers, with her hand on her heart.

Pearl glances at the water glass with her paintbrush in it. "Maybe this *marbun* stuff can help me find him?"

"He doesn't want to be found, Luv," Beryl replies, softly but firmly. "Hard as that is, you'll just have to let him go."

Close to tears, Pearl nods, staring down at her brown feet, not convinced that they'll walk her anywhere near lost family any time soon. She doesn't even know if she wants them to.

Beryl gives her a hug and rises, saying, "Don't dwell on it, Luv. You'll never sleep." She walks out the door, switching off the light behind her.

Pearl gets into bed, feeling bad about the harsh way she pissed off from her mum, who lost her dad when she was young too. Deep down, Pearl doesn't want to lose her; she just had to get free.

She pulls up the sheet and starts sketching a family tree with her finger above her in the dark, starting with a dot high up for Great-Grandma Pearl...

Tribal woman from here, until she got cursed and banished... because she painted me!

Pearl sits bolt upright in bed, suddenly sure that 'seeing' is what causes trouble. I'm living proof of that.

Then *whammo*, Pearl realises, like black is black and white is white right out of the tube. Seeing's not the curse. The prick in the cave did that with his shark tooth!

Pearl flicks off the sheet and switches on the light, suddenly energised. Jumping out of bed, she squirts a blob of black paint at the top of a page for Great-Grandma Pearl and a white blob beside her for Peter Pearler. With her finger, she mixes them and makes an oyster grey blob below them for Nana Raeleen. She squirts a white blob next to Nana Raeleen. Because she married old Ron who left her this roadhouse and a coupla kids: Mum and Aunty.

She mixes in the white and makes two little light grey paint pearls below Nana Raeleen for Marnie and Beryl. Next to Marnie she adds another blob of white for Red and mixes them. 'Cause Mum married Dad and had me...

It seems that no matter how watered down it gets, or scared of the curse they are, all the women in her line 'see'. Pearl looks at herself as the last all-but-white paint blob and impulsively scrunches up the paper.

Seeing's not about colour and it's not a curse!

Pearl paces in the confines of the tatty room, busting to yell. We're pearls! All Great-Grandma Pearl needed to know was how to see stuff without getting killed for it. "And so do I," Pearl tells herself, softly and with conviction.

She sits on the bed and for the umpteenth time wonders why her mum called her Pearl, like a throwback or something. Maybe she just liked the name? Maybe she wanted to remind people that pearls are rare and valuable, although, knowing Mum, she doubts that. Aunty and Mum got traumatised and broken by the curse, Pearl realises. I'm *not* going to let that happen to me! Real pearls are *brave*. They don't clean shitty bed pans and become mini me's to broken mums. Real pearls don't let some bastard's shark tooth curse stunt their ability to see, either.

The thought of Great-Grandma crawling back to the prick who cursed her sends a red-hot bolt of rebellion through her veins. Pearl's *so glad* that she didn't go back for more. Real pearls would rather die than cop crap!

Pearl lies on her bed utterly convinced because every cell in her body agrees. The curse was just a punishment for Great-Grandma's *pearlness*!

Pearl learned at school that a pearl comes from a grain of sand that gets stuck in the sensitive insides of an oyster. The sand never stops irritating it until the oyster grows beautiful nacre around it to protect itself, forming a pearl. She decides that no matter how much it irritates and scares people when she sees stuff, she *has* to blab to try to help them.

And the picture is becoming clearer. She's *not* going to let the women in her line feel cursed, like unwanted bits of grit, just because they see stuff in water.

She beams and jumps on the bed in time with each word, chanting, "We're pearls of wisdom. Seer pearls. *Pearls!*"

Chapter Eight

Pearl wakes still feeling elated about being in a family of seer-pearls. She stretches, listening to the muted machine gun chatter of a Willie Wagtail seeing off a crow outside her room. She steps out shading her eyes, marvelling at the courage of the little black and white bird as it chases the black crow high into the sky.

Eddie waves at her from the windmill platform where he's servicing the rods and engine. His gold nugget glints in the sun.

Pearl waves back and climbs up to watch him work.

"My dad was like you, always fixing stuff," she says. "Big Red, the petrol head. Nothing his tool kit couldn't fix except his love of beer and gold digging."

"He wouldn't be the only one," Eddie good-naturedly replies.

They hear truck gears grinding down and turn to see the pink water tanker rumbling in.

Eddie climbs down the windmill ladder calling inside to Beryl, "Pink's here."

He heads inside, passing seedy-looking Massimo at the servery downing a glass of Yanush's bubbling Berocca. He has a glass of espresso lined up behind it, beside his stovetop espresso maker from his tent.

"Want me to tell her you don't need water now the windmill's fixed?" Eddie asks Beryl in the kitchen.

"Nah," Beryl replies, "I'll sort it."

As Pearl climbs down the windmill ladder, Massimo protects his espresso from the plastic strips as he exits the roadhouse to better see the skinny, pink apparition before him, dismounting from her pink water tanker. Her pink sandshoes lead, followed by pink jeans, belt, t-shirt, wishing stone bracelet and hot pink sunglasses.

Eddie heads out, amused to see Massimo lifting his shades to squint at Pink plucking her pink clipboard from the truck cabin with pink painted nails and pulling a pink pen off it, which she puts behind her ear.

"Gidday, Pink," Eddie says, making Pearl smile.

"Gidday, Eddie," Pink responds as she flicks the plastic strips aside, calling, "You hoo, Bub-ba, Be-ar. Got some water in that kettle of yours?"

Massimo watches Pearl walking past, wearing the same strawberry t-shirt that she was wearing the first time he saw her with her face in the fish tank. He decides that she hasn't forgiven him for kissing her in the caves because she didn't say hello; but she was smiling, so she must still like him, a bit.

Pearl follows Beryl into the office, overhearing Yanush telling Pink, "That tall guy out the front's thinking about taking a room so we should be able to put something toward it soon."

Pearl pipes up, "I've got a fifty."

Yanush waves that away, saying, "For your bus fare home."

"I am home," she retorts.

"This is my niece, Pearl," Beryl tells Pink.

"Saw her coming, the day you ran up your bill," Pink replies, as Pearl rushes out past her.

"I'll make us that cuppa," Beryl replies, heading into the kitchen.

Pink inspects the fish tank, calling through the servery to Beryl, "Waste of water. How'd you pay for *this*?"

"Didn't, duffer," Beryl calls back. "It's the herb garden."

"Oh, yeah," Pink says as she looks outside to where it used to be filled with dirt.

"We'll fix you up later, Pink," Beryl calls through. "Promise."

Before Pink can react, Pearl enters and quietly slips her the fifty-dollar note, pleasantly surprising Pink, who pockets it.

"You lonely in there by yourself, little fella?" Pink asks Curly as she reaches up to trill the water on the surface for him.

Cute Curly starts wagging his tail as he rises, making her smile.

"S'pose it can wait," she calls through to Beryl.

Pink's wishing stone bracelet catches on the glass edge and

falls into the tank.

"Oh no!" she cries out. "Davo gave me that!"

Pearl snatches up a fork and pulls up a chair, leaping on it to try to get the bracelet out before it sinks too far, but she's not fast enough. She looks at the bracelet on the bottom and leans her head close to the surface to listen. BZZT. Pearl jerks back from the surprising sound of an electronic buzzer, glancing at Pink to see if she heard it too. Doesn't look like it.

Beryl comes out of the kitchen sloshing Pink's tea into its saucer at the sight of Pearl back on a chair, leaning over the tank looking at Pink's bracelet on the bottom.

"Don't even think about it – I'll get the long tongs!" Beryl blurts out as she pushes Pink's cup of tea into her chest and races back into the kitchen, calling, "Bear!"

Through the front glass, Massimo sees Pearl on the chair and smugly waves Eddie over to see this, since he couldn't convince him last night that she put her head in the fish tank, no matter how much they drank.

Pearl tilts her head again to listen.

Curly starts sucking on Pink's bracelet.

Pink slaps the side glass, chastising him, "Get off. Off!"

Curly swims backwards, alarmed.

"Aye! Leave him alone," Pearl tells off Pink as she rises on her toes, leaning further in with the fork, but it's just short.

Her fingers strain, her nose is in the water.

Eddie stands staring beside Massimo, just inside the front door.

Beryl is racing to Pearl with the long tongs extended, followed by Yanush from the office.

Pearl flashes them a defiant look, takes a breath, plunges all of her face into the tank and looks trance-like into the water.

"Err," Pink says.

Everyone stares.

Even Curly halts, goggle eyed.

Eddie and Massimo move closer to watch.

In the world of the tank, Pearl bird-arm, frog kicks down, down into a glass-sided rectangle to scoop up the bracelet on the bottom of a glass shower cubicle.

The shower has a view into a mysterious hospital room.

Pearl's arms push up as her feet touch the bottom. She gazes past the white bathroom tiles and pauses as she spies Pink in a hot pink nurse's uniform.

Pink is struggling to lift a bearded paraplegic, with one arm in plaster, off a bed pan. She grunts and presses the buzzer again with her elbow, BZZT, causing the patient to topple on to his broken arm with a yelp of pain.

Pearl screws up her nose as the bed pan upturns its brown sludge all over the bed clothes.

Pink struggles to take the weight off Davo's broken arm, while trying not to gag.

"Piss off," Davo yells, humiliated, waving Pink away with his good arm.

A blur of white nurse uniforms enters to sort out the mess.

Pink steps back, looking hurt and useless in her pink nurse's get up, smarting from Davo's rejection.

Outside the tank, Pink is getting concerned for Pearl. "Do something," she tells Beryl and Yanush. "She's fainted!"

"She'll be right," Beryl replies, nudging Yanush. "We'll look after her."

Yanush steps forward and pulls Pearl out, clutching the bracelet.

Beryl grabs it off her and hands it back to Pink, "There you go. Catch ya next time, Pink."

Pink is affronted. "What's the rush? I haven't even had my tea!"

Pearl jumps off the chair, wiping her face with the front of her t-shirt, busting to tell.

"*Don't!*" Beryl warns her.

Defiant, Pearl asks Pink, "What were you thinking, trying to lift that big, bearded bloke all by yourself?"

Pink glares at her.

Thinking that Pink doesn't believe her, Pearl adds, "The pink uniform was cool though. I'd bugger off too if I had to clean shitty bed pans. Mum wants me to do that job, but there's no friggin' way!"

Pink slams her cup and saucer down on the nearest table, clips her bracelet back on and snaps at Pearl, "Is that your idea of a *joke*?"

Surprised by Pink's aggressive tone, Pearl mutters indignantly, "Saw it in the fish tank."

"Get yourself another water truckie," Pink snaps at Beryl.

"Nah, nah, Pink," Beryl tries to explain with her hand on Pink's arm. "I didn't tell her anything. She's special."

But Pink is wrenching free and storming out of the front door.

Eddie follows her out, also intent on explaining, until he realises that he has no idea where to start, so he heads back up the windmill.

Beryl barges out behind him.

Inside, wowed Massimo approaches Pearl, asking, "You see things in there? People? You saw people in the water of the cave?"

Pearl nods: feeling special beats the shit out of feeling like a cursed bit of grit, again. "First Nation's people," she replies, puffing out her chest. "*Family.*"

"You're amazing – *incredibile.*"

Massimo grabs her hand as he enthuses, "I know free diving. I can teach you how to hold your breath for longer."

Pearl nods, liking that idea, but not him holding her hand.

The water truck roars off, clouding Beryl in dust as she rounds the pumps and halts, momentarily blinded.

Yanush rushes outside to her, blasting Pearl as he passes, "Pack. You're leaving."

He gently guides Beryl inside to the Ladies.

Pearl pulls her hand out of Massimo's, wondering why Yanush is being so harsh. She never meant to hurt anyone, especially not Aunty.

Before she can try to defend herself, Beryl yells from the Ladies, "Get in here, Pearl!"

Yanush puts a plug in the sink and starts trying to splash water in Beryl's eyes to wash the dust out, but she keeps them closed.

As Beryl straightens, Pearl hands her the prescription eye drops that she knocked off the shelf when she first arrived.

Beryl takes the hand towel Yanush offers, presses it on her eyelids and sighs, "Leave this to me, Bear."

Her tone makes it clear now is not the time to cross her. He obediently leaves.

"Aunty," Pearl stresses, "you've *got* to see an eye specialist."

"When I say don't, I mean *don't*," Beryl snaps, ignoring Pearl's concern. "Pink and Davo are good friends of ours."

"Didn't say anything that bad," Pearl mutters as Beryl applies the eye drops, blinks them out fast and slams the bottle back on the shelf.

"Pink's been driving the water truck since Davo, that big, bearded bloke as you so call him, fell asleep one night at the wheel and broke his back, poor fella."

"Fu-ck," Pearl replies.

"The other truckies didn't like it at first, didn't think a woman could hack the Nullarbor run, so Pat went all out Pink as a protest."

"True?" Pearl asks, full of admiration for Pink, who used to be Pat.

"Don't give me true," Beryl snaps, giving Pearl a red-eyed glare. "It's not funny seeing stuff. The things you see about people are sacred to them and you've got no right saying anything about it unless they ask."

"I knew that," Pearl replies sarcastically, kicking the wall.

"It's a curse, Pearl, not a bloody circus trick. I hate it. Bear hates it. Your mum hates it."

"Did Dad hate it?" Pearl asks. "Is that why he left?"

"Don't go blaming the curse for anything Red did," Beryl asserts, softening her tone.

"Plenty of people love it. All the lost sheep looking for answers. They never let up on Nana Pearl 'til the day she died. Bet that's what killed her."

"Was not," Pearl retorts. "Was a shark."

"Yeah? Well, why'd you think she was down there? Probably pressured in by some white bastard wanting answers – or pearls."

"Doesn't anyone know for sure what happened that day?"

Beryl sighs sadly, "Mum knew, but she wouldn't say."

Pearl lets the water out of the sink and rinses it as Yanush yanks the door open.

"She's staying," Beryl insists.

"Bravo," Yanush replies as he clamps a paw over Pearl's hand to twist the tap off.

"Ow!"

Chapter Nine

Both happier now that Pearl seems to have settled down to finish painting the dining room, Yanush heats the chip oil while Beryl puts some water on for the peas.

Pearl is so lost in her thoughts that she doesn't notice Massimo poking his head through the fly strips, pleased to see her on her own.

He seizes this chance to make peace as he approaches, whispering, "I'm sorry I upset you in the cave, *Perla*."

She shrugs it off, wondering why guys always think everything is about them?

"What do you know about free diving?" he asks.

Pearl remembers seeing hot guys diving to great depths without tanks on YouTube.

"I can teach you how they do it, so you can hold your breath for longer," Massimo offers.

"It's like meditation. Do you meditate?"

"Nah. Can't stop thinking."

"Yoga?"

"Boring."

"If you can calm your thoughts, *Perla*, your heart rate will slow and your lungs will not scream for air so soon," Massimo advises. "You'll buy yourself another two minutes, easy. The record is seven minutes. Imagine. Free divers stay so calm that their heart almost stops. Some of them turn blue." His eyes light up as he romantically imagines, "We can practice in the cave."

Wasn't born yesterday, Massimo.

"Painting's my meditation," Pearl replies, returning her attention to the wall. "When I paint, I just think of colours and nothing else."

"Do that when you are holding your breath," Massimo

enthuses. "See colours, think colours, like there are only colours and no need to breathe."

Pearl imagines how that might work. She thinks back to Pink playing nurse in Davo's hospital room, and her perception of the vision changes. It's like she is painting them, not just seeing them, and it looks *amazing*. More amazing was the dazzling light reflecting off the hundreds of silver anchovies that swam around her back in Perth.

"I jumped off a cliff before I came here," she blurts out, "and these tiny little fish, hundreds of them, all started whizzing around me at lightning speed," she adds, spinning on the spot doing fast bird arms. "I was in this silver tunnel going up and I totally forgot I needed air."

"There was a shark nearby?" Massimo asks.

Pearl stops spinning and nods, lowering her arms.

How come he knows that?

"Fish do that to make themselves look bigger when there's an apex predator approaching. They were using you to protect themselves from the shark."

"Huh!" Pearl exclaims. "And all this time I thought they were protecting *me*!"

Beryl comes out of the kitchen with a pile of polony and tomato sauce sandwiches made with white sliced bread.

Massimo frowns at this poor imitation of real tomato sauce, crusty bread and mortadella and heads off before Beryl can invite him to lunch, calling behind him, "Practice, *Perla*. Paint in your head."

*

Pearl practices breath-holding as she paints through the hot afternoon while Bubba and Bear nap. An ocean blue wave crests on the dining room wall, and the arc starts taking shape as Pink's face. Pearl likes how the sunlight blazing in from the front windows gives Pink's blue skin a peachy blush.

Still holding her breath, Pearl calmly steps back to take it in, but sees sleepy Yanush padding out of his room and exhales, hastily stepping forward to paint over it.

"Almost done," she calls to him. "Are we painting the rest or just the dining room?"

"I only bought enough paint to brighten the entry," Yanush yawns. "I hope it sells before the repossessors take it from us. I'll paint 'Priced for Immediate Sale' on the fridge door out the front in the morning," he adds, stretching his muscled arms above his head.

Pearl inhales and holds her breath, trying to calm her mind again, but the thought of repossessors kicking them out is too terrible. How come Yanush's looking so chilled? Has he given up? Is he in denial?

He notices her holding her breath and says, "Bubba can't take the strain anymore and having you here hasn't helped. No more trouble, Pearl."

Still not breathing, Pearl nods and angles outside, allowing the fly strips to slide over her shoulders. She heads down the driveway and exhales as she crosses the highway to sit on a small hillock between the leathery leaves of the drought-stunted Saltbush, red Sturt's Desert Peas and spinifex, trying to work out what to do. She studies the roadhouse, hugs her knees and flicks bull ants off her feet as she tries to meditate. Even with her eyes closed she can't unsee the white caravan she used to sleep in, the petrol pumps she got bathed near, or imagine this run-down roadhouse that she was born in – gone! She opens her eyes and focuses on the top-lit fish tank gleaming through the front glass of the roadhouse deciding... that, above all things, should never be taken from us. Not before giving up all its secrets...

Pearl pulls off the heirloom necklace and squints through the middle of it, angling the shark tooth at the fish tank. She reminds herself that, since she's a seer-pearl, there must be a more important reason why she came than painting a place that will never be hers. Last night's elation about feeling like a pearl is already evaporating. Pearl sits with her blue familiar feeling of loss, the heavy hollow in her heart. She sucks in air again and holds it.

Something is churning in her solar plexus, the beginning

of an indecipherable knowing, a curdling riddle coming from squinting at the fish tank... Unable to shake it, she surrenders. Better to die from a curse than leave a gift unwrapped, she decides as she stands, dusts herself off and heads back across the highway, still holding her breath.

Pearl glances at her watch, timing herself, unaware that Massimo is out the back, quietly knocking on her bedroom door.

"*Perla?*" he calls softly.

No answer. He tries the door and peeks inside to see if she's in there, but she isn't. Instead, he's confronted by the power of her paintings. Massimo steps inside to take a closer look at the terrified toddler staring out at him from the fish tank. And is that young Pearl painted black, wailing about being held back by her black Mamma, both upset by this white man roaring off in his utility? Massimo does a soft whistle, wowed by the raw emotion in this art, by this new First Nation's dimension emerging in Pearl.

Eddie appears in the doorway.

Caught snooping, Massimo flings his hand at the paintings, saying, "Look at this! She is inspired, *searching.*"

Eddie levels his gaze at Massimo.

"What the fuck do you think you're doing in here with Pearl's stuff?" he asks, as he shoves Massimo out the door, ready to take it up with him outside.

But something triggers Eddie, holding him back; the terrified look on the drowning toddler's face deeply disturbs him, until the sound of Massimo's trail bike revving off distracts him.

Neither man sees Pearl, still holding her breath, returning through the front door of the roadhouse with the family necklace in her hand.

Checking her watch, Pearl exhales, pleased that she got to one and a half minutes. She takes advantage of the fact that Bubba and Bear are nowhere to be seen. Quietly, she places a chair close to the tank, stands on it, eases the necklace into the water and drops it, watching it sink. She focuses on the shark tooth glinting at the bottom of the tank, hoping that Massimo's promise of two minutes, if she clears her mind, will be enough to solve this once and for all.

Curly cruises wide, staying well away from the shark tooth in the necklace.

Pearl whispers to the surface, with her face almost in the water, "Why were you down there, Great-Grandma Pearl?"

Faintly, she hears the hush and suck of the sea and a little girl's high-pitched giggling, which reassures Pearl, as she takes a huge, calm breath and pushes her face into the tank…

She kicks down, down to the sea floor to retrieve the necklace and is startled by big heavy boots lumbering past, kicking up sand. She looks up and spies the face of a Japanese pearl diver in his diving suit and brass bell helmet, but he doesn't see her. Pearl bird-frogs up, following his airline, staying calm by painting this vision in her mind. She looks up once more, aiming for the source of the giggles, the bubbly movement she sees beside the wooden hull of a pearl lugger.

Great-Grandma Pearl, a slim, fit young woman like herself, and her young daughter, Raeleen, are swimming.

The giggling five-year-old is kicking like a fish in a bucket, causing hilarity on the surface.

Pearl surfaces in the vision next to her Great-Grandma Pearl, who's treading water, legs wide apart.

She holds up the child's face under her chin, delightedly calling, "Kick!"

Pearl calmly keeps painting this luminous vision in her mind's eye. It is easily the most beautiful thing she has ever seen.

Aboard the lugger, Peter Pearler, dressed in a white cotton suit and pith helmet, is smoking a cheroot, looking fondly on the pair in the water.

He calls down to them with an Irish accent, "Hooray, Raeleen! Keep kicking sweet pea, then all hands on deck will know how to swim."

Pearl is stunned by the crystal-clear beauty of the gaff-rigged ketch. The dark-skinned crew are cleaning oyster shells and tending the airline to starboard. She feels the sudden urge to breathe, but keeps painting, laying down the colours in her mind until the urge calms.

Giggling Raeleen sinks a bit, but soon bobs up, supported by her mother's hands. A little unsettled, she takes a firm grip of the white sparkling necklace floating around her mother's neck and kicks harder, splashing water everywhere. Great-Grandma Pearl lovingly puts the necklace over Raeleen's head as a reward for doing so well with her kicking.

Pearl checks. It's the same necklace that she retrieved from the tank, which anxiously reminds her of what she came here to see. No longer able to stop her heart thumping or her lungs burning, Pearl almost pulls her head out of the tank. But a sudden flash of mottled movement from the murky depths keeps her underwater in this suddenly dreadful place.

Desperately trying to alter the outcome, Pearl re-surfaces in the vision, yelling, "Shark!" but nobody aboard hears her, because Peter Pearler is also yelling, "Shark!"

He throws himself on the deck, reaching both hands out at full stretch to Great-Grandma Pearl, who kicks hard toward him. She thrusts Raeleen up to the safety of her father but cannot reach the rope ladder in time.

The huge Tiger Shark strikes at her waist, violently wrenching her left and right, oblivious to the stabbing boat hooks of the panicked, screaming crew on the listing lugger.

Pearl surges forward to assist, to try to save her ancestor from the sawing jaws of this monster. Her face smashes into the glass as the shark drags Great-Grandma Pearl below the blood red surface, and is gone…

Panicked Pearl is dazzled by a constellation of lights flickering before her eyes, fading fast as she runs out of air and faints in the bloodied water of the fish tank.

Beryl comes out of her room and stalls at the hideous sight of Pearl's head and torso lifelessly slumped in the tank. There's blood clouding the water red like a deadly halo around Pearl's face, the family necklace dangles from her fingers, and her knees have buckled beneath her. All her weight is on the glass edge of the tank, which could break and cut her to shreds at any moment.

Beryl rushes over, wailing, "*Nooooooo!*"

She reaches up with both hands and drags Pearl's head out of the water by her hair, pulling her away from the edge of the tank. But Pearl's dead weight slithers out of Beryl's grasp, and she slides off the chair on to the floor.

Bumping her head on the floor causes Pearl to regain consciousness with a sharp intake of breath.

"Thank God! I thought you were dead," Beryl cries, falling to her knees beside her.

Blood streams down Pearl's face. She drops the necklace, wipes the blood from her nose, looks at the bloody back of her hand and sobs.

Beryl pulls her to her chest in a fierce hug, saying, "Shh, shh. I tried to warn ya. Why don't you listen to me?" She pulls back a little to inspect Pearl's bleeding nose, asking, "What's she done to ya?"

"It wasn't her," Pearl wails. "I hit the glass trying to stop the shark from taking her."

"Why'd you wanna see that for?" Beryl gasps, eyeing the hateful necklace in a watery puddle of blood on the floor.

Pearl looks tearfully at Beryl, "Because you said nobody knew what happened that day, but now we do 'cause I just saw it."

Beryl reels back, breathless with anxiety, "No, no. It's a *terrible* thing to see."

Pearl nods, blubbering, "She was only trying to teach Nana Raeleen how to swim."

Beryl pulls her close as Yanush emerges out of the Gents carrying cleaning gear. He halts, shocked to see Beryl and Pearl on the floor with Pearl's head buried in Beryl's heaving chest.

He sees the blood, drops the bucket and rushes over, calling, "Bubba. Are you hurt?"

Beryl rubs her eyes, replying, "Nah, just got blood in them, can't see."

"What do you mean you can't see, Aunty? Aunty!"

Yanush pushes Pearl aside as he kneels to look in Beryl's eyes, saying, "No blood, Bubba."

"I can't see you, Bear. I can't see anything," Beryl pants.

Pearl snuffs back tears and blood, terrified for Beryl.

Furious, Yanush holds Beryl close and yells at Pearl, "Get out of my sight."

Pearl snatches up the necklace and rushes out of the roadhouse. She hurls it at the roof. It sails high and smashes the brittle neon 'R' out of the roadhouse sign, casting shards down on her as she bangs through the door of her room and slams it. Shut.

*

Yanush lumbers from the pumps to his old sedan carrying two jerry-cans of fuel.

Eddie and Massimo guide subdued and blinded Beryl into the passenger seat.

Pearl rushes over, pushing between Eddie and Massimo to get to Beryl before they close the door.

"Please let me stay, Aunty," she pleads. "I'll look after the place," she adds as Yanush slams the boot and strides around to the driver's side.

Flatly, Beryl replies, "Do what you like. You always do."

Pearl leans in to give Beryl a squeeze as she does up her seat belt, assuring her, "Gunna protect the place, I promise, Aunty."

She looks at Yanush, who's already starting the car, "I'll tie myself to the pumps if anyone tries to take it off ya."

"Just stay away from that tank for your own good," Beryl whispers in her ear.

"Promise, Aunty. Bye, Bear," Pearl replies, sadly disentangling herself and shutting Beryl's door as Yanush begins to pull out.

He winds his window down to call out to Eddie and Massimo, "Thanks, boys. Get some food in if you can. We're almost out."

Eddie waves, calling after them, "Will do. Take care."

Pearl watches them go, feeling vomity-sick like she's twelve again, nauseatingly abandoned.

Massimo raises her hand to wave at the car, saying softly for her, "Get well soon, Aunty."

*

The next day at dawn, Eddie staggers through the servery, dragging a dead kangaroo by the tail, appalling Massimo, who is up early unpacking gourmet supplies from his tent boxes.

"That should impress her," Massimo says.

"Shove over," Eddie grunts. "This bastard's heavy!"

They push each other, spilling into the dining room, now softly illuminated by the rising sun. Both men stop, arrested by an eerie painting on the roadhouse wall.

Pearl's ancestor is in the cave staring down at the shark tooth, falling from the furious elder's fingers into her water basket. His other hand is violently gesturing for her to go.

"Um, ah," Massimo exclaims, "From him, she ran in the cave."

"No, Massimo," Eddie dryly responds, pulling the string to turn the light on above the fish tank, "She ran because she's not into you."

"Funny," Massimo mutters as Eddie moves closer to the wall to get a better look.

His steel-capped work boot rams into something solid under the pile of blue tarpaulin beneath the mural, amid paint mess and brushes.

Pearl sits up fast, like a flick knife. The tarpaulin falls from her shoulders.

"*Madonna mia!*" Massimo exclaims, stepping back.

"Geez, Pearl," Eddie says, smiling down at her, "always full of surprises. Hope I didn't hurt you."

Pearl's confused to find herself surrounded by a mess of her child artist paint tubes, some half-squeezed out on the dining room floor.

Eddie extends his hands.

Pearl lets him pull her up to stand before him. She twists around to peer at the wall.

"I didn't paint that," she says, releasing Eddie's hands as she looks down at her paint splattered, long t-shirt and fingers.

She glances up and sees that he doesn't believe her.

"How could I?" she asks, "in my sleep? I went to bed in my room, not in here."

Massimo is gazing at Pearl with the mural behind her like they are part of a holy fresco. He rushes to kneel before her.

"What're ya doing?" she asks, stepping back.

Massimo pulls out his mobile and takes photos of Pearl with her mural behind her.

"You're amazing, Perla," he effuses as she turns her face away.

Massimo pockets the mobile and rises to ask, "This Indigenous woman. She is... you? No?"

"Course not, Moron," Eddie snaps. "Does she look black?"

Massimo looks at Pearl's ancestor in the mural, "Is she Indigenous, or the perception of an Indigenous woman? Did the stimulus create the dream, or the dream create the image?"

"Wanker," Eddie mutters, heading back to deal with the dead kangaroo in the kitchen.

Pearl replies to Massimo, hoping that he might help her understand, "She was my Great-Grandma Pearl."

"But this is wonderful," he enthuses. "So much dimension. I wish I... I have no idea what is in my blood. The Huns swept through Venice, raping and pillaging... and there have always been rumours of a Moroccan trader."

Pearl zones out, unable to deal with it.

Massimo sees that she's not listening.

Undeterred, he adds, "You must be exhausted, *Perla*. I will make you *frittata*."

"Not hungry," she mutters, closely looking at what she recognises as her style in the mural, maybe even her best work.

Try as she might, she can remember nothing about getting up in her sleep, retrieving her old paints from under the bed in the caravan and painting this. And why those old paints when she brought some with her? None of it makes sense. She rubs the nauseous, hollow feeling between her breasts that started when her dad left: the exact place where the spirit of her great-grandma swam through her to scare away the shark. No wonder, Pearl thinks, after being ripped apart by that monster that left little Nana Raeleen motherless...

Being cursed, banished, or abandoned leaves the same hole in your heart, she realises. Sadly, she wonders if the abandoned little girl inside her painted this with her kiddie paints.

Pearl busies herself packing up the tarpaulin, brushes and paints, trying not to answer that. As acutely uncomfortable at it makes her feel, she knows what Great-Grandma Pearl felt and what Nana Raeleen felt.

Being banished or abandoned makes us feel like we've got no bones, no place to belong to, no soul. And that feeling follows us around every single day until we abandon ourselves.

Tears well in Pearl's eyes. The angry elder in the mural mists before her.

Is there no end to the hurt that men make?

Eddie calls to Massimo from the kitchen, "I could go a couple of fried eggs, mate. Hold the Ratsak."

"Please go," Pearl calls behind her, dashing away her tears with the back of her hand. "Piss off for a couple of days."

"I will take a room here," Massimo offers, approaching, "to help pay their bills."

Pearl casts her hand at the door without looking at either of them, "Both of you, just go."

Something in the flat decisiveness of her tone tells them that she means it.

The men look at each other and leave in separate directions: Massimo to his trail bike, leaving his box of gourmet supplies on the bench and Eddie to Norm's, dragging his dead roo behind him to butcher over there.

*

At Country Downs, Eddie chisels hard to remove the last of

Norm's bathroom tiles, sending shards flying.

Norm shelters behind the shower curtain.

Ray stands in the doorway wearing his flying goggles, trying to keep up with the latest news.

"If Beryl and Marnie are a quarter, Pearl's only an eighth," Norm tells Eddie. "Hardly worth a mention, mate."

"That's not what I'm telling you, *mate*!" Eddie snaps.

"Touch-y," Ray replies.

"Pink told us about her tank prank," Norm puts in.

Eddie downs tools. "Wasn't a prank. She saw stuff about Pink because her head was in the fish tank with Pink's bracelet... I think."

"Reckon it's the dreamtime?" Norm ventures.

"Nah, more psychic," Ray reckons. "Beryl always said there's a bit of Irish in 'em," he adds, flashing a gap-toothed grin at Norm. "Wonder what she'd make of me?"

"Don't go there," Norm mutters, stepping back as Eddie hauls out the bathtub, grunting.

Eddie straightens, asking Norm, "Got a special possie for this?"

"Nah. Take it to the tip."

Since the nearest tip's a few hundred kilometres up the road, Eddie double-checks, "You want me to take this to an *actual* tip?"

"Chuck it off The Bight for all I care," Norm mutters.

Ray spreads his hands, "Reminds him of his ex-wife."

Eddie nods, but his mind's still on Pearl. "Last night," he tells them... "she painted her Aboriginal ancestor in your cave on the roadhouse wall... in her sleep!"

"So," Norm muses, "She's a psychic, Aboriginal, Irish artist?" He turns to Ray, "Reckon he's in love?"

"Reckon so," Ray replies.

*

Massimo is floating in the blue-white cave water in his speedos and head torch, gazing up at the ancient handprints on the wall, trying to become as peaceful as a meditating guru in a float tank. But he can't get it out of his head: Yanush's love song.

He starts to sing, giving in to the emerging feelings he has for Pearl with his voice echoing eerily around the cave, "The one love you'll find, once in a lifetime."

Pearl must be 'the one', he decides, wondering how best to show her.

Chapter Ten

Ray pulls up in the red Australia Post van in his postie's uniform, but Pearl's in the shower and doesn't hear the nasally sound of the old van arriving. He lugs in a big box, drops it by the door and goes back for another one.

Pearl wanders out barefoot in her floral dress with wet hair and halts, staring at the van and the delivery. She leans over to read the label, surprised to see it addressed to her.

Ray returns with the other box and sees her for the first time. Pretty, he thinks as he puts the box down. No wonder Eddie's gone ga-ga over her.

"Special delivery for Pearl," he says, extending a hand to shake and offering her his best gap-toothed grin. "I'm Ray," he adds as they shake. "Sign here."

"I didn't order anything," Pearl replies, not accepting the pen. "There must be some mistake."

"No mistake, Luv, unless there's another Pearl at this address. You only have to sign for it, not pay for it."

Pearl signs, asking, "Does it say who sent it?"

Ray checks.

"Porter's Paints, Fremantle."

Mum! Wow! Is she making up? Showing me that she is happy for me to be an artist?

Love floods Pearl's heart with forgiveness as she dashes into the kitchen to get a knife to cut the tape.

Ray heads back to the van and returns with a bunch of window-enveloped bills, which he places on the second box.

Pearl cuts the first box open and pulls out one litre exterior acrylic paint tins in all the primary colours, beaming like it's Christmas.

Ray stands before her mural looking most impressed, saying, "Wowza! Amazing work."

Pearl makes a mental note to paint over the old kiddie paint with this top shelf stuff. She cuts open the second box, making the mail slide off and discovers tins of black, white, green, blue and brown.

Brilliant!

She gathers up the mail, opens one, sees the yellow overdue sticker and scrunches it.

"What do ya know?" she mutters. "Phone's gunna get cut off."

"Better pay up," Ray warns. "Out here, once it's cut off, it could be weeks before they'll reconnect it."

He sneaks a look at the fish tank and proffers Pearl the rabbit's foot on his key ring, asking, "Can I have a reading?"

Pearl glances at this cheeky bald postie and wonders how he knew. Word must be getting around.

"Not sticking my head in there again," she refuses, shaking her head. "Promised Aunty. And I'm not psychic, just cursed."

"Don't believe that gumph, do ya?" he asks, with the rabbit's foot still extended.

"Dunno," Pearl replies, ignoring it. "Can't see the future, just bad stuff from the past."

Ray twists the rabbit's foot off his key ring and drops it in the fish tank. Plink!

"Please, Luv," he begs. "I'll pay for it."

Pearl gives him a filthy look. "The name's Pearl."

"Please, Pearl, I need to know something important," Ray pleads.

Pearl crosses her arms. "No."

While Pearl's distracted by Curly zeroing in on the rabbit's foot, Ray makes his escape.

She calls after him, "Hey! You get that out!"

"Catch ya later, Pearl," he yells behind him as he bolts out grinning. "Mail's gotta get through."

Pearl glares at the tiny bubbles escaping from the sunken rabbit's foot, but Curly wags his tail, liking them. She scowls, remembering what Aunty said about Great-Grandma Pearl,

"Probably pressured in by some white bastard wanting answers."

Some white bastard like Ray?

"It's a curse, Pearl," Aunty said, "not a bloody circus trick."

Too right! Not today. Not happening.

She walks into the office, picks up the phone and punches in Marnie's number fast, before she changes her mind.

"Hi, Mum. Just called to say thank you so much for the paints," Pearl rushes. "If the line goes dead it's 'cause the phone's getting cut off."

"What paints?"

Pearl freezes, wondering if Marnie's shitting her. She waits, but there's no 'just pulling your leg' or 'glad you like 'em', just the sound of a lighter flicking on and Marnie doing the draw back. Pearl is tempted to hang up, but she needs to know something super important.

"Have you heard from Aunty?"

Marnie exhales in Pearl's ear, saying in her flattest voice, "They're running tests. She's still blind, thanks to you."

Pearl is too gutted to answer. She hangs up, convinced that to her mum she will always be a bit of grit and nothing will ever change that.

How could I be that stupid? To even imagine Mum capable of sending me paints? … Well, somebody did.

Pearl shelves that thought as she resolutely pulls a chair up to the tank, pushes hard on the top with both hands and hoists herself up to sit on the edge. She swings her legs into the water. Her toes clamp around the rabbit's foot, but, just as she goes to flick it out, her bum slips from under her. Pearl falls in over her head, causing water to splash over the sides of the giant tank.

Alarmed, Curly skirts around her to avoid getting squashed.

*

Later that night, Eddie pulls in, determined to have it out with Pearl about how come every time they get close she pushes him away, but he sees that Massimo has beaten him home. His trail bike is parked outside the room next to Eddie's with lights on inside.

Eddie grits his teeth, resisting opposing urges to deck Massimo if Pearl's in there with him, or to just give up and head straight back to Norm's. Pearl's bedroom door opens with no lights on inside. Eddie's relieved. Assuming that she's heard his ute idling outside, he hopes that she is coming out to talk to him. He switches off the ute, jumps down and walks toward her, but she walks right past him. He sees that she's sleepwalking barefoot in a clean long t-shirt, past the pink bathtub on the flat tray of his ute, without even noticing it. He follows her into the roadhouse.

Massimo's curtains part in time to see them. He quietly follows, not realising that Pearl is walking in her sleep, until she starts mixing some of her new paints on her palette in the dark inside the roadhouse. Massimo looks at Eddie and flashes a hand in front of Pearl's face.

She doesn't notice.

Eddie pulls the string to switch on the globe above the fish tank.

She doesn't blink.

Massimo studies the mural, pleased that she has used the paints he bought her to enhance it while they were gone.

In a trance-like state, Pearl starts painting a new section of mural.

Eddie shrugs at Massimo, like he knew she was weird, but this takes the cake.

Massimo paces over to hiss at him, "What do you expect from an Indigenous oracle?"

Eddie holds a finger to his lips, hissing back, "Shh!"

As the mural develops through the long, silent night, Eddie busies himself with bagging up the roo meat he butchered at Norm's and stacking it in the deep freeze. When that's done, he casts about looking for things to fix, starting with the air conditioner and then the vacuum cleaner, neither of which he dares to switch on in case it wakes her.

In silent awe of Pearl, Massimo takes her paintings from her room and tacks them up on the freshly painted walls with tacks from Yanush's office. He sticks fifteen-thousand-dollar price tags on the bottom corners, made from yellow post-it notes. Pleased, he makes himself a short black, while watching this amazing *signorina* painting in her sleep, but the new section of mural emerges slowly and the coffee cannot keep him awake. Massimo rests his heavy head on his hands on a dining table to watch her and falls asleep.

*

As the pink hues of dawn begin to stream in, Eddie and Massimo stand before Pearl's new work. At full height and stark naked in the mural, with the exception of a footy scarf, is Ray, standing in front of Norm with his arms crossed and legs apart. Norm is waving him aside from his possie on their ratty sofa, annoyed because Ray is obstructing his view of the footy on TV.

Massimo is amazed at the perfectly telling looks on their faces. Norm is depicted as the dominant-avoidant, alpha-male and Ray the feminised, attention-seeking desperado.

Troubled, Eddie guides Pearl, still asleep and clutching her paintbrush, away from the mural and back to her room.

Massimo would not believe it if he did not see it with his own eyes. He makes himself a fresh coffee, amazed that such an inspired work could be painted while one's sleeping. He wonders if it is he who is dreaming as he sees Norm entering the dining room.

"Gidday, mate," Norm calls through the servery. "Got you working, have they? I've got a bit more work on for Eddie too. Is he about?"

Norm flashes a look around the roadhouse and halts, gaping at Pearl's rendition of himself and naked Ray on the wall.

He yells through to Massimo in the kitchen, "What the fuck… does she think she's doing painting me and Ray on the wall like *that*? Where is she?"

Eddie rushes to stand in the entrance to prevent Norm from heading out the back to nab Pearl. Nobody notices the mail van pulling up behind Norm's truck outside.

"Doesn't know she's doing it, mate," Eddie begins, approaching Norm. "Does it in her sleep. Told ya."

Norm pushes Eddie aside, still yelling, "Well she can bloody well undo it quick smart with her eyes open. I'm not being branded a poofta!"

Massimo swaggers out of the kitchen sipping his espresso, which he puts down, advising Norm, "It's a divinely inspired work. Personalities and moralities should never intervene."

Norm's face goes beetroot with fury.

"Cut the crap, Massimo," Eddie snaps, worried that Norm will blow a gasket. "It's his life."

"Too right," Norm blusters, as he stoops to pick up a wide wall paint brush.

Massimo races over and tries to wrestle it off him.

Ray has entered behind them, witness to all of this.

"Find it offensive, do you?" Ray asks Norm.

"It's not you that I find offensive," Norm snaps, winning the tug of war with Massimo for the paintbrush. "It's her, putting it up there."

Ray replies, nonplussed, "Footy grand final ring a bell?"

"Yeah, we lost," Norm grunts, throwing the paintbrush on the floor.

"Fuckin' hopeless," Ray snaps, casting a hand at himself in the mural, "You never notice."

Norm infuriatingly asks, "Notice what?"

Ray stands before Norm, legs apart, crossing his arms, just like himself in the mural.

"Me," he replies. "I don't mind if the world knows."

"That we're *mates*!" Norm interrupts, glancing at Eddie, "That's all there is to it."

Ray rolls his eyes and tsks, "I've had it with your stupid self-deceptions, Norman."

"Fine, then pack your bags and fuck off!" Norm bellows, unwittingly giving Ray the same banishment gesture as the elder behind him gave Great-Grandma Pearl in the mural.

Sleep-befuddled Pearl stands outside the fly strips, peering

94

incredulously through them at naked Ray on the wall that she must have painted and all the chaos that's causing. She stumbles back to her room.

Ray crumples into a ripped red dining chair as Norm barges out and roars off in his truck.

Not knowing what to say, Massimo places his espresso before Ray.

"Ta," Ray says. "I can't believe he's kicking me out after all these years." He asks Eddie, "Was he serious?"

Eddie screws up his face and shrugs like it doesn't look good.

"Never thought the day would come," Ray tells himself aloud. "Mail's definitely not getting through today. I'd only drive off the road or crash the crop duster."

Massimo takes pity on him, saying, "I am sorry for your loss. Would you like to use my tent?"

Ray takes a pensive sip of the espresso, tearfully responding, "That's so kind of you, Massimo. Could you come with me while I get my stuff and some drinking water? I don't know what he'll be like when I get there."

"*Si, certo.*"

Pearl lies low in her room and pretends to be asleep, waiting for the testosterone party of trouble she's stirred up to piss off before re-entering the roadhouse… As soon as they go, she picks up the phone in the office to call the hospital, but the line's dead.

Pearl slams down the receiver, takes the last coins out of the cash register, untacks her ridiculously high-priced paintings off the wall and jogs up the highway with her paintings, toward the enemy roadhouse that killed off all of Aunty's and Yanush's trade.

*

Ian, the weedy boss of the monstrosity roadhouse, scribbles zeros off Massimo's fifteen-thousand-dollar price tags on Pearl's art, reducing the price to one hundred and fifty dollars a pop.

Completely out of her depth, Pearl ignores his argy-bargy about what percentage of commission he'll take when they sell.

It's a different air-conditioned world in here with its well-lit food displays and uniformed staff chirpily serving tired motorists. A red-headed dad accepts keys to one of the luxuriously appointed rooms outside, making Pearl's heart ache for Red for the first time in ages. She follows the wealthy family outside. The parents unload swanky suitcases from their Jeep, while their teenagers laugh and jump in the fenced-off swimming pool.

Pearl trudges to the hot, fly-ridden phone box near the stinking bins and calls Midland hospital, where Yanush took Aunty.

Finally connected to Aunty's room, Pearl speaks fast in case her coins run out, "Everything's fine, Aunty. The phone's cut off, but Massimo's taken a room. I'll get some of it changed into coins so I can call again later. I'm trying to sell my paintings to get the phone put on again. Have you seen the eye specialist?"

The pay phone begins to beep. Pearl anxiously pushes in her last coin, firing off questions as soon as Aunty answers.

"What do you mean one eye's good, but the other one's got cancer! Did you know it had cancer before? Who gave you the eye drops?"

Pearl listens and interjects, "You can't let them take the blind eye out, not without a second opinion! What about the good one? Well, bloody make sure. Sorry Aunty, it's all my…"

The phone cuts off.

"Argh!" Pearl yells, slamming the receiver into its cradle.

She flicks flies off her as she fights her way out of the stinking hot phone box.

Through the gleaming glass front of the air-conditioned monstrosity, traumatised baby Beryl stares out at her from the dining room wall with the reduced price yellow post-it note tacked to her arm. Pearl feels bad about leaving her in enemy territory and guilty about flogging family secrets. She trudges away with sleep-deprived, gritty eyes and leaden legs. Being responsible for so much bad stuff happening makes her feel like she's tracking mud all the way back to Aunty's.

*

There, Pearl finds Eddie approaching the fish tank, with less water in it from her rabbit foot fall in, holding a blue bucket and hose. She races into the kitchen for a glass of water and turns on the tap, but nothing comes out.

She rounds the servery, rushing up to Eddie. "We're out of water," she tells him. "Please don't drain it. Curly needs it. Didn't mean to stick my head in, just slipped."

"On purpose," Eddie assumes, pushing the hose into the tank.

"Not on purpose," Pearl insists, pulling the hose out. "You try living with a curse and see how you like it! What I don't get is how come it makes me paint in my sleep!"

Eddie's gaze softens as Pearl's hardens, realising that it definitely wasn't Eddie who sent her the paints.

"Pearl," he says. "I just fix windmills. There's enough desalinated drinking water in the tank while I fix the plumbing. It's not that I don't care about you. But I care about my mates too. It's for your own good. Just stirs everyone up."

Pearl nods, defeated, muttering, "Gotta get Curly out first."

Eddie looks around, asking, "Where's your paintings? Massimo reckons they're worth something."

Pearl climbs on a chair and scoops Curly up in the bucket, puts the bucket on a dining table, climbs down and slumps into a chair beside it.

"Took 'em up the road to sell. Aunty's got to have an eye out, and it's all my fault."

Eddie sits opposite her, struggling with a decision. He pulls his gold nugget necklace over his head and places it on the table between them.

"Here," he offers. "Send it to the Perth Mint. Should fetch a fair whack, enough to get the phone back on and some food in. Sorry to hear about Beryl. I've been staying here to help them out instead of getting paid for windmill repairs up the line, but I have to go soon."

Pearl looks at the nugget, undecided.

Eddie puts the bucket on the floor, glancing at Curly circling warily inside his new blue prison, staring unhappily up at him.

"He can keep his condo on one condition," Eddie says. "No more sticking your head in."

"I promised Aunty that I wouldn't, but *she* still needs me," Pearl pleads, casting a hand at Great-Grandma Pearl in trouble with the elder in the cave part of the mural.

Eddie scoops up the nugget, "No probs. I'll keep it."

"No, no," Pearl rushes, "It'd be a good help at the right time. Thanks, Eddie."

Eddie looks into Pearl's eyes, takes her hand, puts his nugget in the centre of her palm and closes her fingers around it. Pearl doesn't look away. He leans over the table and kisses her. They rise together as their kiss intensifies. Eddie pushes the table aside. They press against each other.

Norm walks in, mumbling to himself, at first not seeing Pearl behind Eddie, or their kissing on the other side of the fish tank.

"There you are," Norm calls to Eddie. "Fuckin' Ray's making a song and dance about clearing out, *and* he's refusing to let me paint over that mural!"

Norm rounds the tank and sees Eddie and Pearl reluctantly pulling out of their kiss.

He glares at Eddie and heads out, calling behind him, "Nice to know who your mates are!"

Eddie rolls his eyes at Pearl and shrugs, palms up, as he follows Norm out.

*

Eddie and Norm watch Massimo and Ray as they load Ray's battered suitcases into Ray's 'mail mobile'.

They head off, Massimo in the mail van and Ray bouncing down the drive in the crop duster.

Eddie glances at disgruntled Norm, who resumes his smoko on the veranda as if nothing's happened.

Nearby, Bonox the bull twitches a fly off his ear like he's listening.

"Had a word with her," Eddie begins.

"More than a word," Norm mutters, "from what I saw. Bit bloody late. Pink's left Davo stranded in hospital, Beryl's blind and black, and we're gay. Who's gunna be next?"

Eddie thinks carefully before responding, "Wouldn't matter if you were. Wouldn't change anyone's attitudes around here… We'd still be mates."

Norm screws the lid on the thermos like he hasn't heard, but Eddie sees that he's relieved.

"Got any spare jerry cans?" Eddie asks. "Can I use your phone to order in some plumbing?"

Norm waves a hand at his front yard junk heap, muttering, "Yeah. Help yourself."

*

Ray is sitting in a pink bathtub on the edge of the world. The vista of the wild Southern Ocean is so majestic that it brings him to tears. He waxes lyrical to Eddie as he flicks his hair back, sending a cascade of salty droplets through the cloudless sky. The sound of waves drumming dramatically against the cliffs of The Bight far below intensifies his feelings.

"Only you could rig this up in bastard Norm's ex-wife's bathtub," Ray tearfully declares. "You're a true mate, Eddie, and Massimo's been marvellous too, lending me his tent."

Eddie ignores Ray's nakedness as he unties his rope, rock and bucket rig from the winch, throws it in a steel box on the ute's flat tray, opens the driver's door and gets in.

"Glad you like it," he calls to Ray. "Catch ya."

"Know who else'd love this?" Ray calls after him. "Pink."

Chapter Eleven

Pearl's eating a mid-morning breakfast of vegemite toast, staring at the fish tank, struggling with competing impulses. As much as she's driven to solve family mysteries, she's also repulsed by all the trouble it stirs up. Her promises to Aunty and Eddie weigh heavily on her conscience. She didn't paint anything last night, she reasons, because she didn't stick her head in the tank yesterday; and just as well as she slept for twelve solid hours. It stirs her up just as much as everyone else, so Pearl decides to give it a rest for a while as she flicks in some flakes for Curly.

She packs all of her paints and brushes back in the boxes the new ones came in, climbs on a dining chair, hefts them into one of the high storage cupboards above the servery and padlocks it. Pearl stares at the key in her hand, wondering what to do with it to stop her sleepwalking-self from using it.

A huge, white removal van pulls in with 'Kalgoorlie Speciality Markets' written on the side. It stops right outside the front door, blocking most of the light. Pearl's heart does fast, anxious flips as two heavy looking dudes jump down from the cabin.

They unload fridge trolleys from the back of the van and wheel them in.

Pearl frowns and pockets the key, remembering what Yanush said about repossessors as they prop their trolleys against the servery on either side of her.

"We're closed," she tells them, aiming for a big voice that comes out too high-pitched. She nervously glances at the trolleys, adding, "Pretty sure we didn't order anything."

The bogan-looking driver gives her a sharky grin, revealing uneven teeth and cruel eyes as he tells her, "I'm Vince. This is Doof. We've come for your contents and your cash."

"What?" Pearl squeaks, jumping off the chair, which she instantly regrets because now they're both leering down at her, looking built, intimidating and proud of it.

"You heard," Doof replies, breathing foul cigarette breath in her face.

Vince hands her a letter from the finance company and starts unloading the last of the drinks from the dining room fridge, helping himself to a Coke while he's at it.

Pearl's gaze darts to Eddie's gold nugget necklace that she left on the servery, relieved that they haven't noticed it. But they might at any moment.

"Hey!" she yells. "You pay for that! What are you doing with our fridges?"

Vince takes a gulp out of the can, forces out a gassy burp and asks, "Can't you read?"

He puts the Coke on a dining table, saunters into the kitchen and starts throwing their meagre freezer supplies on the floor: a half empty tub of vanilla ice cream, bagged kangaroo meat and the last of the burger rolls.

Pearl rushes to put them on the bench divider, while snatching up Eddie's nugget and shoving it in her pocket, but then she thinks they might make her turn out her pockets. She anxiously glances around for a safer place.

Doof lifts the cash register, jangling it, muttering, "Fuckin' empty."

Pearl sidles past the fish tank, drops the nugget in the corner and rushes to confront them.

"You leave that alone!" she snaps, consulting the letter. "Says nothing here about…"

"Whole thing's about money, Luv," Vince sneers, enjoying her discomfort, as Doof walks out with the cash register. "It's called debt."

"And we're debt collectors," Doof adds over his shoulder, talking sarcastically slow like she's thick, as he returns to wheel the kitchen fridge out, followed by Vince with the freezer.

Vince looks around for any other white goods, as Doof doubles back for the dining room drinks fridge, asking him, "Want the deep fryer?"

"Is it empty?"

"Nah, full of filthy fat," Pearl spits out, relieved that she packed Massimo's supplies in the built-in pantry, along with a bottle of vodka that Yanush accidentally left in the office.

"Leave it," Vince tells Doof, as he starts stacking the red vinyl dining chairs, "These retro tables and chairs are worth a bomb – collector's items. I'll get that bedroom cleaned out." He juts his chin at the open door into Beryl and Yanush's room. "You start on the rooms out the back."

Pearl is torn between dashing after Doof to grab her stuff and protecting Curly and the nugget in the tank. She winces, immobilised by Vince's disrespect, as he hurls Bubba and Bear's stuff from the bedside tables and their clothes from the wardrobe on their pink chenille bedspread, which he bundles up and drags on to the floor.

He inspects the mattress but leaves it – too old and stained.

Good, Pearl thinks, relieved.

Vince faces her and sits on it, bouncing as he pats the mattress beside him, saying, "Might be good for *something*."

"In your dreams," Pearl spits out, raising her middle finger, desperately wanting to run, but she holds her ground because she told Yanush: "I'll guard it, Bear. Tie myself to the pumps if anyone comes to take it off ya."

Pearl doesn't know how long she stands sentinel beside the fish tank, shocked by being ripped off in broad daylight. Angry at the awful way Vince chucked Bubba and Bear's belongings on the floor like they were nobody, she's pretty sure Doof won't want any of her stuff, either. She tries to lose herself in breath holding, mentally repainting the mural, but soon feels sickened by a toxic miasma of self-recrimination.

As Vince flips the mattress to look under it for stashed cash, she thinks, Fat lot of good I am as a guard. Just lucky Vince isn't dragging me in there to be raped.

Doof returns to tell Vince, "The beds out the back have all had it and the cupboards are built in. No TVs."

"Yeah, this wardrobe's a piece of shit too," Vince replies,

pretty sure that what they've collected will more than cover this place's pissant debt.

He scoffs in Pearl's face as they leave, "Make sure the rest of this shit's out by the tenth of next month, including you."

Pearl exhales with relief as she watches the removal van rumble off. She slides down beside the TV stand and sobs.

*

As the sun sinks, Pink bathes in Norm's pink bathtub on the cliffs, wearing nothing but a pink shower cap. She pours the last of her pink champagne into her pink plastic mug, singing, "Sav-iour all the human re-he-heh. She in-ven-ted med-ic-inal com-pound," but Pink can't go on.

She holds her mug up to salute the pink striped sky and cries out, "Miss you, Davo."

*

The sun sets over the desert horizon as Ray and Massimo arrive back at the roadhouse in Ray's mail van.

Norm and Eddie also pull up in Norm's truck.

Ray leans toward Massimo, "Thanks for all your support. You've got a great big dago heart, Massimo."

Massimo takes Ray's face in his hands and gives him a double cheek farewell kiss, saying, "*Forza!* Stay strong!" as he steps out of the van.

Ray nods and squares his shoulders to look over at Norm, who's looking back, not happy. With a triumphant little twitch threatening to lift the corners of his lips, Ray realises that Massimo's goodbye kiss was not lost on Norm.

Eddie gives Norm a supportive punch on the shoulder as he gets out of Norm's truck.

Eddie and Massimo glare at each other. Norm and Ray do likewise from inside their vehicles, when Pearl comes out, holding out the letter from the repossessors for Eddie and Massimo to see.

"They took *everything*," she wails, casting a hand at the empty dining room, with only the fish tank on the big old TV stand left in the centre.

Eddie urgently looks into her eyes, asking, "Did they touch you?"

Pearl shakes her head and hands him the letter.

Massimo heads inside, distressed to see spaces on the wall where her paintings were hanging.

"*Dio mio*," he exclaims, casting a hand at the wall. "The paintings!"

"They didn't get them," Pearl says as she walks past him to the servery.

Eddie retrieves an old, steel ice box from his ute. "This'll do for a while," he says, piling in the defrosting roo meat.

Pearl picks up the half-empty ice cream tub, which holds only warm sludge now and leaves the buns on the bench. She grabs Yanush's bottle of vodka from the pantry and pours half of it into the melted ice cream. She takes a big slug from the tub and passes the bottle to Massimo.

He holds the bottle out to Norm and Ray as they shoulder past each other in the entry. Eddie hands the repossessor's letter to Norm. Ray jumps up to sit on the servery bench beside Norm, leaning in toward the letter, with his legs dangling like a little boy's.

"Twenty-eight grand's owing," Norm grumbles. "Second hand stuff doesn't fetch much."

Astounded, Massimo asks, "They cannot take this place from Beryl and Yanush for only twenty-eight thousand Australian dollars, can they?"

"Only!" Pearl replies, hugging the ice cream tub. "Who's got twenty-eight grand?"

"We would have sprung 'em the cash if they asked," Norm says.

Ray agrees, "Too right."

"Too proud," Pearl says, wiping more ice creamy booze off her lips, eyeing the blood oozing over the sides of Eddie's old ice box.

"Bin it," she tells him. "It'll only go off."

Ray looks at Norm and then at Eddie.

"Got enough kero?" Norm asks.

Eddie nods and smiles at Norm as Ray jumps off the bench to stand beside him. Like men on a mission, they head for the door. Eddie hefts the ice box but sees his gold nugget in the corner of the fish tank. He puts down the ice box to face Pearl.

"What's my nugget doing in there?"

"Best way to protect it," Pearl says, but she sees that he doesn't believe her.

"Find out what you needed to know?"

"What?"

"Pretty cheap, breaking our deal like that," Eddie snaps.

Pearl slams the ice cream bucket on the servery, yelling, "If that's what you think, you can bloody well keep it. But that water's staying in!"

"Fine!" Eddie yells back.

He rounds the kitchen counter, yanks out a drawer and grabs the long tongs.

"Careful of Curly," she warns him, as Eddie stands on his toes in his work boots and reaches in, getting an ear wet.

He pulls out the nugget by its leather strap, floating suspended above the nugget.

"Didn't hear anything," he says as he wipes the ear with his shirt and pulls the wet nugget necklace over his head, "Mustn't be an oracle like you!"

He heads out, throws the ice box onto the back of his ute and roars off toward Country Downs.

Massimo hands the ice cream bucket back to Pearl, saying conspiratorially, "He has a secret, *Perla*. Get something from his room and have a look."

Pearl shakes her head, "Nup. Promised not to."

"Who did you promise?"

"Aunty. And Eddie."

"Why?"

Pearl walks unsteadily to the mural, slurring, "Dunno what their problem is." She adds, "It all started with her," waving her hand at her ancestor, "Wait here. I'll show ya."

Pearl weaves out to the caravan, wrenches the door open, snatches two framed photos off the dusty mattress and backs out, almost stumbling down the steps. She heads back into the roadhouse and pulls Massimo by the sleeve to look at the sepia photo of all hands gathered on the deck of the pearl lugger.

"That's her in real life: Great-Grandma Pearl when she was young. Beautiful, eh? After she hooked up with that white fella, Peter Pearler-wanker. He's the one who put curse prick's shark tooth into the middle of the necklace he made her. Dunno why. And that's Nana Raeleen, their kid, when she was little."

She shows him the other photo of the old roadhouse with scrawny Raeleen and her two toddlers standing outside. "Here's Nana Raeleen grown up with Mum and Aunty when they were little. Aunty only ended up with this roadhouse because Peter Pearler brought Nana Raelean here to Great-Grandma Pearl's country." She points again to Peter Pearler and Great-Grandma-Pearl gazing at each other on the pearl lugger.

"They were in love," Massimo interjects with a sentimental sigh. "So easy to see. How lucky they were to have found each other – the Pearler and his Pearl."

"Real lucky," Pearl slurs, "since she soon got taken by a shark. Plus, he already had a white wife and kids. At least he cracked poor Nana Raeleen out of the mission that he shouldn't have put her into and brought her here, which got her married and kids." She points again to the roadhouse photo. "First, it was hers, then it was Aunty's, 'cause Mum wanted me to go to school in Perth, then it was gunna be mine, 'cause Aunty's got no kids, but that's not gunna happen now, eh?"

Massimo gazes around the derelict, empty roadhouse with its holy fresco of a mural and fish tank and says, "My family has been in Venice for six hundred years. All of our buildings are sinking into the sea with all of our marriages rotting inside. Everyone sneaks off to make love with other people, and we call that love too." He picks up the lugger photo for a closer look. "These people knew how to love. Yanush was right to leave Europe forever to stay with Beryl."

Something is beginning to agitate at the edge of Pearl's vodka-sozzled brain, something about the Pearler already being married and the Venetians all sneaking off to cheat.

Massimo's blurry face confirms it as he moves in close, murmuring, "It is not unknown for a man to love someone other than his wife, *Perla mia*. Someone who understands him."

Pearl pulls back, asking, "Have you got a wife?"

Massimo hesitates. "We are separated in distance and in time," he replies, watching Curly weaving and ducking in the fish tank.

"How long?"

"Not so long."

"Cassandra."

"Cassandra does not understand me," Massimo hedges. "She, she…"

Pearl pulls his face around to look her in the eyes, "She is waiting for you back in Italy?"

Massimo lifts his chin to free himself from her grip as her gaze intensifies, replying, "Maybe yes, maybe no."

Fucking hell! At least Eddie's single!

"You think it's *right*?" she asks, "Letting us believe she's just a girlfriend who pissed off?"

Suddenly tired, so tired of everyone's shitty deceptions, Pearl feels like nothing computes. Everyone hides something? What is *wrong* with people just being honest? Don't I deserve to be told the truth?

Massimo sees her shutting down, almost asleep standing up, hugging the ice cream bucket to her chest. He is just in time to catch her as her knees begin to buckle.

"Oh, sorry," Pearl says, sliding the ice cream bucket back on the bench, "Must have nodded off." Weaving out with the photos under her arm, she slurs, "I'll sleep in the caravan. Alone, married Massimo. Oh, and thanks for the paints. Still not gunna sleep with ya."

Massimo reluctantly lets her go. He wonders what Pearl would discover about him if he put something of his in the fish tank and instantly thinks better of it. She might hear what Cassandra said when she left, about him only ever loving himself, and a variety of other women when it suits him, which was, of course, an exaggeration. No, he decides, he cannot risk that. Besides, he does not believe that is him anymore, because this time it's different. He has *feelings* for Pearl. Massimo vows to keep trying to make her understand how rare and precious those once-in-a-lifetime feelings are – starting tomorrow.

Chapter Twelve

Bonox licks Eddie's face, abruptly waking him at dawn.

Eddie pushes him away, causing a pile of leaky empty beer cans to fall off Norm's sagging veranda couch, where he crashed out. A couple of raucous kookaburras laugh from the junk heap, amplifying the pain in his head. Eddie wipes the bull slobber off his face with his t-shirt and rises, causing more empty cans to clatter onto the veranda. He pats Bonox, takes a leak in a cracked toilet on the junk heap and returns to feel under the remaining cans for his keys.

Eddie drives slowly to the roadhouse, remembering the decision that Norm made him make last night, about Eddie getting up early, grabbing the stuff he left in his room at the roadhouse and doing a runner before Pearl wakes. Since he totally blew it by taking his nugget back, a quiet escape still seems like the best course of action in Eddie's beer-sozzled brain. It's all coming back: what drunken Norm told him last night in no uncertain terms.

Firstly, Norm assured him that he's not an Indian giver, so the whole oracle trip must've done his head in if he took that nugget back; and why did he give it to her in the first place?

Secondly, Eddie doesn't need drama, drama, drama, nor does Norm. He isn't letting Ray come back yet. Everyone was happier before Pearl blew in with her tell-all tank pranks.

Thirdly, Norm stated *categorically* that all women are trouble, with Ray not far behind. For the umpteenth time, Eddie heard how Norm's ex-wife, Diane, nagged him into tarting the place up as a tourist ranch, only to piss off with the sleazy property developer!

"Fuck that for a picnic!" Norm added, as if he wasn't stamping his point enough.

Fourthly, and finally, Eddie should just forget about Pearl and get stuck into his windmill servicing work up the line. He's contracted to keep those windmills turning.

Eddie barely remembers fifthly, because with Norm there is never a finally. He sifts through his memory until it comes back. Fifthly was about him not making much traction anyway, with dago Massimo always sniffing about. Eddie remembers pointedly reminding him that he might have made more traction if Norm hadn't bloody interrupted their last kiss!

The sixth point Eddie also barely remembers is swimming through his head on a king tide of beer in the wee hours. But he remembers that it was important, like the real reason that he's flogging a dead horse, according to the gospel of Norman...

Trust! That's it, like the concrete you pour in your house foundations. If it dries cracked, it's too fucked to build on.

Driving with alternating hands, Eddie presses his temples to try to ease his hangover headache. He didn't tell Norm that his trust in women went south years ago, right after his mum's suicide. The thought of being vulnerable to that much hurt again chews up his guts. And he didn't tell Norm how his heart armours up as soon as he starts to feel for someone either, 'cause there's nothing he can do about that... except hope that it won't. He didn't trust Pearl when she said she didn't stick her head in with his nugget, and he definitely doesn't trust that she's into him enough not to sleep with Massimo. That's six good reasons to piss off, Eddie thinks, as he quietly pulls into the roadhouse.

Rain falls on his windscreen, which beggers belief. Every time the weather man predicts the chance of a shower out here, he thinks, it means bugger all chance of a shower. He gets out of the ute, squints up at the cloudless sky and sees it.

Eddie rushes to bang on Pearl's bedroom door, yelling, "Pearl! Get up quick! Tank's sprung a leak!" He scampers up the water tank ladder, pulling off his blue t-shirt which he jams against the leak, still yelling, "Pearl!" from the tank stand.

Equally hung over, Pearl steps out of the caravan rubbing her eyes. She sees water spraying on Eddie's windscreen, which suddenly stops. Pearl squints up and sees wet, bare-chested Eddie, pushing hard against his t-shirt to quell the leak. She scrambles up the tank ladder to help him. Eddie pushes her hands against his wet t-shirt.

"Keep up the pressure!" he yells as he races down for tools.

Water soon starts squirting through. As Pearl adjusts her stance to put more pressure on, a jet squirts through Eddie's t-shirt right into her eyes, momentarily blinding her. She opens them and sees that she's on a different tank stand on the dust-dry desert plain. Even though this is not the ocean, fish tank, or even the shower, Pearl automatically holds her breath. Her heart races as she looks down and sees Eddie wearing the dry blue t-shirt that she is still pressing into the leak at the roadhouse... so, the water in her eyes must have passed through his t-shirt, she realises.

Pearl considers blinking a few times to rid herself of this uninvited vision, but she doesn't because she suspects Massimo is certain that Eddie's hiding something, and she wants to know what it is.

Eddie is kneeling beside a prospector who is slouched, seated with his long legs straight out and his back against the base of the stationary windmill. His battered Akubra hat has fallen forward, obscuring his face. Eddie pushes the prospector's leg with his boot. No reaction. He gingerly pushes the prospector's hat back to peer under the brim at his face and jerks back from his decaying head.

He sees something gleaming on the dead man's chest: a gold nugget the size of a cherry, dangling off a leather strap. He stares at the nugget for a long, decisive moment, pulls his Swiss army knife out of his pocket and cuts the leather strap.

Pearl cringes as she watches Eddie pull at the strap to steal the gold nugget from the dead man; the same nugget that he retrieved from the fish tank yesterday. The prospector's hat slides off.

Pearl sharply inhales and howls like a wounded animal as Eddie slams the hat back on Big Red's fly-blown head.

Desperate to escape this new horror, Pearl squeezes her eyes shut, reeling back in a cascade of water from the released t-shirt and begins to fall off the tank stand.

Eddie races up, dropping tools, lunging for her, yelling, "*Nooooo!*"

He hugs Pearl to him at the last moment, knees buckling with relief. They slide below the squirting jets on to the wet tank stand.

"That was close," Eddie says softly, "Shh, shh, your heart's thumping, eh? Breathe."

Pearl stares into his eyes like he's despicable, unsettling Eddie, who rushes to apologise.

"Sorry I didn't believe you about the nugget," he says, pulling off the necklace.

Pearl jerks back, revolted by knowing where it came from – her dad's decomposing corpse – causing uncomprehending Eddie to extend it closer to her, with a desperate urge to kiss her.

"Here. Please, Pearl," he begs. "I trust you. Please take it. It's yours."

Those words strike Pearl in the heart as she realises that it *is* actually hers, since her dad found it prospecting. But she doesn't want to get it from Eddie corpse-ransacker. What she wanted was to find her dad *alive*.

"Don't touch me," she gasps, wrenching out of Eddie's arms, rising through the spraying water to stand over him, yelling, "I know what you did!"

Eddie gets up, wrings out his saturated t-shirt and re-jams it against the hole in the tank. He turns, pressing his back hard against it, leaning forward to glare at Pearl, who glares back.

Massimo wanders out of his room, yawning loudly as he looks in Eddie's ute.

Eddie yells down to him, "Bring us those tools, quick!"

As Massimo grabs the fallen tools, Pearl scrambles down, rushing past him, breathing in fast, anxious gasps.

She runs up the steps of the hot caravan, slams the door and shoves the family photos off the unmade bed, gutted because nothing she knows about her family ever ends up being true. The hole of hurt in her heart widens and deepens, all but swallowing her up.

Defenceless, Pearl curls up on the bed like a foetus and sobs for the loss of a dad who didn't abandon her forever like she thought. He was likely sending her money via Piss Pot right up until he died. What kills her is that he might have *actually wanted* to know her growing up. And now he never will.

*

Eddie's mind's eye replays what just happened with Pearl. He never thought she would judge him, looking down on him, yelling, "I know what you did!" when he tried to give her back the nugget. Stealing that was the lowest thing he's ever done, Eddie admits to himself, which is why he didn't want her finding out. But why did she turn so *suddenly*, helping him one minute and hating him the next? Why did she cry for hours then not want to talk about it? Norm was *adamant* about him pissing off back to work, but Eddie still feels beholden to try to talk it out with Pearl in case of a misunderstanding. Not that she's making it easy.

Leak fixed, he gulps tank water, still feeling like the walking dead. He watches puffy-eyed Pearl trudging up the highway with Massimo, who waited outside the caravan calling for her to come with him as soon as her wailing stopped.

Pearl might be walking, but Massimo's doing all the talking, Eddie would be willing to bet. You can't cry like that, like he cried after his mother drowned, and come out chatty.

Convinced that Norm was right about him flogging a dead horse, Eddie packs his stuff in his swag, but can't bring himself to throw it in the ute. It's easy for Norm to tell him to piss off, but Eddie can't, not without trying to sort it out. He distracts himself by fixing the plumbing and anything else he can lay his hands on while waiting for them to get back.

*

Stomping about on the tin roof, Eddie can just see them returning in the shimmering late afternoon heat haze, carrying supplies and eating ice creams. He leans over with the spare globe to replace the broken neon 'R' in Roadhouse, spots Pearl's necklace inside and lifts it out. Eddie replaces the bulb, but the flickering 'R' only comes on in fits and starts and the other letters remain dimly lit.

He climbs down the ladder and waits at the pumps to offer Pearl her necklace back, but she walks right past him.

Massimo gives him a you-win-some-you-lose-some smug look as he follows Pearl inside, leaving Eddie standing there like a fool, still holding out the necklace.

Trust? It's not fuckin' automatic, Norm, Eddie thinks, as he lowers the necklace, but at least he tried. It's still eating him alive that stupid-fool-he trusted Pearl not to stick her head in the fish tank with that nugget, which she obviously did, resulting in, "I know what you did!" so he shouldn't have trusted her. And all he was doing was trying to help!

A loud truck honk blasts away his ruminations. Eddie stares at the 'Swim for Your Life' banner on the front of a semi-trailer slowly approaching on the highway.

A glass-sided swimming pool sloshes past on its flat tray, with a man in speedos inside, swimming across the desert to raise awareness for health and fitness. A support vehicle follows with its young crew waving at Massimo, who's sprinted out to see the swimmer, waving back.

"*Madonna mia*!" Massimo exclaims. "Only in Australia."

Inside, Pearl is peering out of the front window looking non-plussed. Nothing really surprises her anymore.

Still hung-over, Eddie trudges in, looking green around the gills, as he places her necklace on the servery bench.

He turns to face her, but, maddeningly, Massimo materialises through the fly strips.

Pearl averts her gaze to the fish tank, back wall mural and front wall. 'The Swim for Your Life' rig has prompted her to imagine how the roadhouse could look like a giant fish tank, especially at night with the lights on, if the back wall was all mural and the front all glass.

"Should take out that front wall," she mutters, more to herself than to either of them.

"Yeah, why not?" Eddie replies, buying time by unscrewing the front plate off the switch to the globe flickering above the fish tank. "The roof'll fall in, but who cares?"

"What have they got to lose?" Massimo calls through the servery from the kitchen, where he's making himself an espresso.

Eddie glares at him, replying, "You personally? Nothing."

"It's not your place, either," Pearl snaps at Eddie, "so shut the fuck up."

Abuse now? Eddie thinks, as he squeezes a stale bun on the bench and drops it. What he really needs is a big greasy burger, a pile of fries and no drama. He grabs his keys, too hot and hung-over to handle more of Pearl's madness or silent treatment, and it's too late to piss off for work.

He calls behind him as he heads to the monstrosity, "Hope you've got plenty of torches. Generator's on its way out. Have fun destroying the place, kids."

*

The sun is setting by the time Eddie returns, heading straight for his room to crash.

Pearl picks up the necklace and turns to Massimo, "Do me a favour?"

"Anything," Massimo answers, gazing into her eyes.

She hands him the necklace, beckoning for him to follow her out to the caravan, finds its padlock and keys inside, turns and hands them out to Massimo.

Scowling at the necklace, she asks, "Can you lock me in, please, Massimo, and hang this on one of those high pot hooks in the kitchen so I can't reach it?"

Massimo nods, lingering on the top step of the caravan, reluctant to lock her in.

"I could stay with you, hold you," he offers, "never let you go… to your mural all night."

Pearl feels so tempted to be held, comforted, but not by married Massimo or thieving Eddie. She sees Eddie watching from his room and tilts her chin up to Massimo, who takes her in his arms and kisses her. Pearl kisses him back, but her focus in not on Massimo. Nugget-nicking Eddie is still spying from his room. If them kissing makes him puke, good!

"Fuck!" Eddie curses, drawing his curtains in disgust.

He was right not to trust her, *again*!

Pearl pulls back from the kiss, feeling an overwrought, sickening mix of revenge and sadness.

"What'd you do that for?" she asks Massimo, pushing him down the caravan steps. "Lock me in and if I get out, shoot me," she adds, slamming the door.

Massimo tries to padlock her in, but the padlock is rusted open, as broken as everything else in this place. He hooks it through the steel eyes on the caravan, making the door as good as locked from Pearl's side. He hopes that Eddie will not discover it unlocked from the outside if he returns later, wanting again to fight…

He does not know what Pearl and Eddie fought about this morning because Pearl would not say. Despite her still feeling hurt, or maybe because of it, she allowed him to kiss her just now. Not the most passionate of kisses, Massimo concedes, but it's given him hope, because she let him kiss her *despite* knowing about Cassandra.

Massimo hopes his English words were good enough when he described his marriage to her as a battlefield, when they walked to the new petrol station. *Si, certo,* exactly that: the marriage of opposites who only fuck and fight. Massimo believes that he would never fight with *Perla*. And it would never be fucking, he's convinced, because with her he only wants to make love that honours his feelings and transcends the boundaries of his toxic marriage.

But there is a problem, Massimo thinks on the way to his

room. It takes patience to solve the mystery that is Pearl, but endless time he does not have, because his tourist visa will expire soon…

He doesn't want these precious days to end, because every day he discovers more about her, which is igniting the buried, better parts of himself. *Mamma mia!* Who would have thought that this adventure holiday, which he so 'selfishly' dragged city-loving, shopaholic Cassandra into, would end with him falling in love with an artistic, Indigenous oracle?

Massimo decides to make his move tomorrow. He whistles, happy that Eddie has improved his chances by fighting with Pearl and ruining his own chances. His whistling soon turns into Yanush's love song melody as Massimo heads to his room.

"Love takes practice," he recalls Yanush saying. He repeats it triumphantly as he passes Eddie's room, adding, "Lots of practice."

Chapter Thirteen

Massimo wakes early. Gazing at the pink light of dawn blushing through the tatty curtains, he stretches, amazed about how fantastic this desert place makes him feel. It's another world. *Anything* is possible here, far from the affectations and pretensions of his life in *Venezia* with Cassandra. How fortunate that she threatened divorce and flew home. It's what he's always wanted, prayed for, but never dared to hope for: the chance to find himself in forgotten places… where, miraculously, his 'one love you find once in a lifetime' happens to live. Discovering Pearl's visions and defending her art is now his passionate mission, adding so much meaning to his life. What *joy* it brings him to be her sole supporter, even though she never asks, perhaps because she never asks.

Massimo quietly lets himself out of his room, pleased that Eddie's room is still in darkness. He removes the unlocked padlock from the caravan door, happy that the interior lights of the caravan are also off. He rounds the front of the roadhouse, rolling up his sleeves, eyeing the front wall like a worthy opponent. Savouring delicious anticipation about what a surprise it will be for Pearl, Massimo strides to Eddie's ute and lifts out a sledgehammer.

With his long legs planted firmly apart, Massimo takes a wild swing at the front wall with the sledgehammer, looking like a leggy shot-put thrower, a drunken praying mantis. He smiles as it connects well enough to take a large chunk out of the wall with a satisfying crash! Massimo widens the hole with a few more blows, continually glancing for signs of Pearl coming out of the caravan, marvelling at how well she must be sleeping. He climbs through the waist-high hole like a cat through a cat door, pulls the sledgehammer in and prepares to strike again from the inside.

Just as he does, sleepy Pearl rises in the kitchen, behind the servery.

"Hello, Houdini," Massimo says with a stupid grin, putting the sledgehammer down to wipe the sweat from his eyes. "How did you escape?"

He spies a tiny bit of curtain flapping in the breeze in the caravan window and waves a finger at Pearl like a naughty girl.

"Through the window, eh?"

Exhausted, Pearl shrugs, thinking she must have, as she eyes the paint under her nails with distaste, leans through the servery and sees the storage cupboard doors above open with the key in the open padlock, dangling. Both turn to the mural to see what she painted: Eddie, kneeling before dead Big Red, pulling the gold nugget from around his neck.

"Has Eddie seen it?" Pearl asks anxiously, with her heart thumping in distress.

Massimo shrugs, answering, "*Non lo so.*"

Pearl races through and shakes the last ten litre tin of wall paint by the mural, hoping there's enough left to paint over it. Desperately, she tries to open it with a screwdriver, but Massimo sits on the tin.

He turns her hips toward her great-grandma in the mural and puts gentle pressure on Pearl's shoulders to make her sit before her work.

He leans over to say in Pearl's ear, "*Bis Nonna* knows best. She is guiding you, helping you see that Eddie is a criminal. I knew he had something to hide. It is your best work, *Perla mia.* You cannot paint over it. Who is this dead man?"

"Dad," Pearl breathes, curling forward in pain just from having to say it.

Massimo rises, pushes the tin back and slides down to sit behind Pearl and hug her, asking,

"What happened, *Perla mia*? Did Eddie kill him?"

Outside, Eddie approaches, suspiciously eyeing the hole in the front wall. He flicks the fly strips aside, only to be confronted by the love birds canoodling again. He takes in Pearl's new addition to the mural and glares at her, at the two of them in cahoots.

Pearl tries to stand, but Massimo holds her tighter, condemning Eddie, "Yes, that is you, *animale*. You and your shameful secret."

Eddie furiously snatches up the sledgehammer.

Massimo rises fast, expecting trouble.

Pearl jumps up and anxiously rushes between them, while appealing to Eddie, "I never put my head in with that nugget. And I locked myself in the caravan so I wouldn't paint *that*!"

"With him!" Eddie yells, trying to wrench the sledgehammer free, but Massimo is not letting it go.

"No! Idiot!" Pearl yells.

"Liar!" Eddie yells back.

Pearl shoves him in the chest, "Where is he?"

"Who?"

"Dad."

"Pearl's papa," Massimo declares, casting a hand at Big Red in the mural, slumped at the base of the windmill. "You killed him."

Eddie takes a long look at the dead prospector, beginning to understand.

"Where is he?" Pearl asks, quieter this time, suddenly close to tears.

"Oh my God, Pearl, I'm so sorry," Eddie says. "I didn't know he was your dad. You and I hadn't even met." He yells at Massimo, "And I'm not a fuckin' killer!" as he wrenches the sledgehammer off him and staggers back.

Pearl scowls at him, not knowing what to believe. Why won't he say where Dad died?

Eddie cringes at himself stealing the nugget in Pearl's shaming mural, but even worse than that, now he feels responsible for the death of her dad.

He paces with the sledgehammer, anxiously reasoning, "How was I supposed to know that he had broken down out there, dying of thirst because I hadn't fixed the windmill?"

Eddie yanks off the hateful nugget and throws it in the fish tank, yelling at Pearl, "He's had his revenge and gotten his gold to ya, so find him yourself!" His voice breaks as he yells, "It's not right what you're doing with that fish tank that I made ya, and it's gotta stop!"

All his anger, shame and grief combine as Eddie wields the sledgehammer in a wide arc and crashes it into the fish tank, breaking the glass with a sickening smash!

The water gushes out of the tank onto the shattered glass on the floor as Massimo wrenches the sledgehammer off Eddie, slamming them into the front wall, which cracks, starting to give way.

Panicked Curly flip-flaps, cutting himself on the glass. Pearl rushes to rescue him, cutting her foot, but it's too late – he's shredded.

Eddie pushes off the collapsing wall and fights his way out through the fly strips.

Pearl squats in shock, staring at the bleeding lifeless fish in her palm, with her own blood staining the water flowing across the floor toward the mural. She's oblivious to Eddie barging out of his room with his swag, chucking it in the cabin of his ute and roaring off.

Massimo eyes the gold nugget gleaming in the bloody water as he lifts Pearl and carries her to sit on the servery bench, trailing big drops of blood. He winces as he eases the shard of glass out of the arch of her foot.

"*Mi dispiace, Perla*," he says softly, eying the silent tears that roll down Pearl's cheeks while she strokes dead Curly, looking glassily up at her from her palm.

*

Driving as far away as fast as possible, Eddie decides to start his run in Kalgoorlie and work back. The highway windmill and tank stand soon appear where he and Pearl got sprung kissing and jumped off the bus. Eddie accelerates, but at the last moment brakes. The back wheels slide around, creating an ochre dust cloud as the ute skids to a halt. Eddie punches the steering wheel, jumps down, slams the door and strides to the tap to splash water on his face.

There, he sees Pearl's discarded water bottle half full of sludgy water. He scowls as he picks it up.

Climbing the ladder, Eddie thinks about all that's happened since they met and how fast it went to shit, thanks to Pearl being a shaming oracle with a thing for sleazy wogs. On the platform, he unscrews her water bottle, averts his nose from the stench and pours the putrid water on the dirt far below.

The wind picks up, making the windmill turn. Eddie looks across at the smoothly turning blades and sadly exhales, unable to forgive himself for the one that he didn't get to in time. He drops Pearl's bottle and heads back down, wishing that they'd never met.

From now on, he decides to concentrate on one thing and one thing only: systematically servicing every bloody windmill up the line, before some other bastard dies of thirst and ruins his life.

*

Sad and exhausted, and with her foot wrapped in a blood-stained tea-towel, Pearl carries what is left of Curly to her room out the back. Carefully, she lays Curly on her bedside table and falls like a stone onto the bed, sleeping in her clothes through the heat of the day.

While she sleeps, Massimo disposes of the smashed fish tank glass, bashes down the rest of the front wall and clears away the debris.

As the sun sets, Pearl wakes, feeling refreshed for a couple of seconds until reality kicks in. She can't believe that Eddie yelled, "Find him yourself!" instead of telling her where to find her dad's remains. She shudders at the thought of breaking it to her mum, who will refuse to pay for the funeral if and when they find him. Sad as it is, knowing that her dad's dead takes some of the sting out of believing that he just didn't want to know her. His smile never lied. In this moment, she realises that she'd rather know than not know everything about the family, because not knowing *sucks*.

Pearl waves a fly off Curly, wondering what sort of send-off would be right for a goldfish who was more than just a fish. He had been her constant companion since she first got to Perth, her little bestie with a wicked, waggy tail. Tears cloud her eyes again. Pearl splashes her face with some water from her water bottle, remembering how she used to play with Curly all the time in his fishbowl in her annexe. She feels sorry about not playing with him much here, since Eddie fixed up his fish tank condo and she started seeing stuff in it.

She hops around the front with Curly in her palm, amazed to see the front wall all but gone and relieved that the roof hasn't fallen in. She wonders what Aunty and Yanush will say to Massimo about his handiwork, *if* they get back before the repossessors return.

"Big job," Pearl tells Massimo, noticing how the focus of the place is now all on the mural, just as she imagined. "I don't know how to thank you."

"You're a visionary, *Perla mia*," he says, rubbing white rubble dust out of his hair. "I must shower," he adds, opening the door to the Gents. "Ray came with Norm this morning to say that Eddie went back to work on his windmills," he says with a shrug. Grinning, he confides, "I don't think Ray is sleeping in my tent anymore either."

Pearl gently places Curly on the servery bench, not surprised to hear that Eddie took off, but the familiar wrench of partings tugs at her. It's more the wrench of not finding out where her dad died than Eddie leaving, especially since she hasn't forgiven him for stealing the nugget or killing Curly… but her churned up feelings say there's more to it.

She unwraps the bloody tea-towel off her foot, sees that the cut has stopped bleeding and hops into the Ladies for a shower. She lets the warm water wash over her with her weight on the good foot and her eyes firmly shut, focusing on those feelings…

Again, she hears Eddie yelling at her about what she does with the tank not being *right*. What is right? *Normal?* Who is he to tell her what's right? There's nothing normal about it. Ever since Great-Grandma swam through her, she's been seeing stuff, painting it, blowing everyone's cover and breaking taboo to suss out her family's secrets. And she's *over* being told not to! Awake or asleep, she paints the shame of things that all have done, because that is what she is shown. It's obvious to Pearl: all wounds bleed before they heal. Why be shown stuff if revealing it does them no good? People only hate her for showing them up. Is any of it right? *Is painting it right?* Pearl feels something opening inside her to make space for 'no'. Little lights spark behind her eyelids.

No?

She doesn't have all the answers or know exactly what right means, but she's willing to keep following her feelings until every step she takes feels right.

Pearl turns off the shower and opens her eyes, feeling like a pearl again, more able to handle whatever happens next. Tank or no tank, if there's more to find out, she will. And she will *not* be shamed out of painting it by anyone who tries to stop her, unlike what happened to Great-Grandma Pearl. It all started with her cave painting and Pearl's going to finish it, 'cause her feelings tell her that is what will make things *right*.

*

Pearl limps into the roadhouse in clean clothes with a fresh tea-towel around her foot and pulls the string to turn on the flickering light above the space that was the fish tank.

She backs out to see it lit up at night from the pumps, which is pleasing, because she can see how the roadhouse would look like as a giant fish tank if her mural were complete.

Wet-haired Massimo waves to her from the kitchen in a clean shirt and jeans, where he is boxing up some of his pantry supplies.

Pearl waves back, still squinting at the mural, imagining how

124

her finished work could tell the story of her family in the watery way of her visions, if only there was time.

Massimo lifts Pearl's family heirloom necklace down off the high pot hook and walks out to her. He fastens the necklace at the nape of her neck.

Pearl shudders as the shark tooth grazes against her clavicle.

He holds her shoulders tenderly to reassure her and pushes the gold nugget into the back pocket of her jeans.

"We are going out to dinner in my tent," he says, offering her his arm as he helps her into the passenger seat of his four-wheel drive.

*

At Massimo's camp, Pearl waits for him to find some knives and forks in his tent. She stands under the stars in a circle of kerosene light, listening to an Italian singer crooning from his phone in words that she cannot understand.

Massimo backs out of his tent, puts the knives and forks on his folding table and holds her. "You've changed my life," he says, breathing her in, not noticing how distracted and sad Pearl is.

"Never thought it would be Dad who found me," she sighs, wriggling out of his embrace.

"This is a magic place," he responds, "where anything is possible. Perhaps we all came here to learn something… I must go back to *Italia, Perla*. My tourist visa has nearly expired."

Pearl nods, secretly relieved.

"I'm leaving, too," she says. "Gunna check every windmill on the Nullarbor until I find Dad and bury him."

Massimo looks in her eyes. "Come with me to *Venezia*. Leave the past behind."

Pearl holds his gaze. "This is my place," she replies.

"Do you have any idea how beautiful and exceptional you are?" Massimo asks. "From the first moment I saw you with your head in the fish tank, I knew. My world awaits you, *Perla*."

Pearl steps back, saying, "I don't love you, Massimo. Not like that. Besides, you're already married."

Massimo cannot disguise his disappointment. "You love Eddie?"

Pearl doesn't know how to answer that, except with the truth.

"I think I understand him, the shame he must be feeling," she replies, "so much shame that he laid some of it on me."

Massimo crosses his arms.

"It is terrible, what he did."

Pearl nods sadly, "He didn't make Dad leave. He didn't bust the windmill. He just didn't get there in time to fix it."

"But the nugget."

Pearl holds a finger to Massimo's lips.

"He killed Curly," he insists, taking Pearl's hand, placing it over his heart, but seeing in her stoic, unflinching gaze that he has lost her. In barely a whisper, he adds, "Don't let him crush your gift."

"I should go," Pearl says, withdrawing her hand, peering past him into the dark bush. Faintly, she hears waves crashing against the distant cliffs on the edge of the world.

"I will drive you," Massimo offers, but Pearl is already hobbling toward the roadhouse, unconcerned about getting her clean t-towel bandage dirty.

"Nah, thanks anyway," she replies. "Need to clear my head."

Massimo rushes to hand her the lantern, which she accepts and keeps walking. He stands awhile, watching her go in the glow of the lantern and then his head hangs in defeat.

"Goodbye my love," he whispers as he crawls into his tent.

Pearl glances back, sees him gone and changes tack, circling wide to head down to the caves.

*

Inside the cave, Pearl stands calf deep in cold water, holding the lantern high to illuminate the ancient handprints. She knows exactly what she must do. Balancing the lantern on a ridge jutting out from the limestone wall, she removes Great-Grandma Pearl's necklace and smashes the shark tooth against the wall. It snaps off into her hand. Pearl looks long and hard into the blue-white water she is standing in, splashes some in her eyes and holds the broken shark tooth up to the wall, gleaming jagged and white in the light of the lantern, commanding the past to reappear.

Again, she sees the angry elder throw the same shark tooth at her great-grandma with the severest of banishment gestures. The shark tooth lands in her water basket.

Pearl lunges to remove it as her ancestor asks, "*Marbun?*" but her hand goes straight through the basket.

Again, the elder does not deny it. Resigned to a fate that Pearl cannot change, Great-Grandma Pearl's head hangs with shame and grief as she sloshes right past Pearl, trudging toward the rocky cave opening carrying her water basket.

Pearl glares right into the angry face of the elder, who cannot see her. "Your curse ends now, bastard!" she yells, throwing the broken shark tooth back at him, making her blink and him vanish.

Bits of shark tooth land in the shallow cave water. Pearl stamps on it with her good foot, picks up the lantern and pulls the family heirloom necklace back over her head... but something still doesn't feel right.

On her lantern-lit scramble up the rocks to the cave's entrance, Pearl pauses to ponder, fingering the space in the necklace where the shark tooth was...

If Great-Grandma Pearl saw me jumping off that cliff, if she painted that and got cursed for it, then she painted it for a reason. Did she paint it for me to see? And when she saved me from that shark back in Perth, did she save me for a reason?

Pearl climbs out of the mouth of the cave and halts, asking herself: is it done?

Have I reversed the curse?

She shudders at the memory of poor Great-Grandma Pearl trudging past her again with that shark tooth in her water basket, and the answer is *no*! Pearl had to do something to rid herself of the curse, but feels that there is more she must do to save her ancestor in the past...

Pearl limps back to the moonlit roadhouse, punctuated by the flickering 'R' on the roof, holding Massimo's extinguished lantern. She pauses by the pumps, taken by the way the flickering light above what once was the fish tank eerily illuminates her mural in the dark. The space below the light globe painfully reminds her of the loss of Curly, which makes her more aware of the pain in the arch of her throbbing foot.

Everyone has gone now: Aunty and Yanush, Eddie and Massimo. Even this roadhouse will go soon. Pearl feels their absence in the hollow in her heart that will never be filled because it's all her fault. Acutely, she feels responsible for the loss of Aunty's eye, for exposing everyone's shameful secrets and the pain that caused each of them. No, Pearl decides, painting that stuff is so not fuckin' *right*!

She enters, via the demolished wall Massimo only smashed through to please her, but nothing pleases her, does it? All she knows how to do is abandon any love she finds, just like her dad, who abandoned her.

What would he make of himself, exposed like that, as a rotting corpse set upon by Eddie? What would he make of *her*? It makes her feel worse than hollow, sick that she has done nothing for him to be proud of.

Pearl bows her head to give her dad the minute's silence she should have given him sooner and, in her mind, begs his forgiveness for the fucked-up person she's become, the bringer of nothing but trouble.

Pearl opens her eyes, turns away from the mural, gently scoops up dead Curly from the servery bench and hobbles back toward the cliffs. The sun begins to glow over the horizon behind her, but Pearl doesn't notice. Her back's to the light.

As she hobbles along the winding track, drawing ever closer to the cliffs and the pounding waves far below, Pearl glimpses a pink bathtub through the blue-grey saltbush and blinks, wondering if it's a mirage. She presses on and finds the bathtub full of sea water with a pink shower cap by its side.

"Ah, Pink," she sighs, shaking her head. "Only you could think of this."

She passes the bathtub to look down into the dark waves with their dawn pink-tinged froth, like a giant bubble bath. There is no buoyancy in the thought, no urge to fling herself into the sea that she usually feels when she's so close to cliffs. All Pearl can feel now, like a lump of undigested pie in the middle of her chest, is nauseating sadness. She brings her hand up to kiss dead Curly and then drops him over the edge, watching with tear-smeared eyes as his tiny dot of orange flutters in the updraft and then plummets into the turbid, melancholy sea.

Chapter Fourteen

"Are you awake, *Perla*?" Massimo calls through the open window of the caravan early in the morning. "I've come to say goodbye."

He lifts the curtain to peek in and sees that she's not in the caravan. He dares to open the door of her room a little to peer inside, but she's not there, either. Massimo frowns, concerned and unhappy that he didn't insist on driving her back here last night, especially with her cut foot. He rushes inside the roadhouse and sees that she is not sleeping in the kitchen or at the base of her unchanged mural, but his extinguished lantern is on the servery, where dead Curly was...

Dangerous scenarios rush through his head in quick succession: a venomous snake may have bitten her; she may have fallen off a cliff in the dark; or drowned in the pristine, but treacherous, cave water. Did she sleepwalk onto the highway and get hit by a car? Massimo's catastrophizing is rudely interrupted by Pink's water tanker repeatedly honking as she hurriedly pulls in and parks at the pumps. Fearing the worst, Massimo rushes out to see why Pink is honking so many times like something's wrong. Could she have picked up injured Pearl from the side of the road?

He skids to a halt as he sees a yellow-Lycra-clad, penny-farthing rider pedalling past on the highway, followed by a bunch of happy Down's Syndrome kids, walking and waving, also in yellow Lycra and matching runners.

Pink issues a last blast of her horn and jumps down smiling from the cabin.

To Massimo's further amazement, she is no longer dressed in pink.

She runs back to the highway waving cash, jogging alongside the slow-moving support bus with a 'Downs Just Do It' fundraising decal on the side. Pink pushes her cash through the windows to the cheering Down's Syndrome kids inside who are on a break with their carers and the reserve penny farthing rider.

Puffed and pleased, Pink strides back to Massimo with her hands on her hips. She doubles over to catch her breath, straightens, takes in the destruction of the front wall and flings an arm at it, glancing up to the tanker's cabin.

Breathlessly, she asks Massimo, "What's happened? Looks like a bomb hit it. Where's Beryl?"

"In hospital," Massimo replies, for the first time noticing that Pink has a big, bearded passenger riding with her in the cabin.

"Don't envy her that, do we, Davo?" Pink calls up to him as she goes over to his side of the tanker and unloads a wheelchair. She turns back to Massimo, asking, "Have Beryl's eyes been playing up again?"

Massimo nods, wondering if his eyes are damaged too. Was that a real penny farthing bicycle being ridden at the front of the procession of happy little yellow people?

"Just stopped by to say sorry to Pearl for making such a hullabaloo about my bracelet," Pink says. "Is she inside?"

Massimo sadly shakes his head.

Davo opens the passenger door and uses a hydraulic hoist to let himself down into the wheelchair.

How good they are together, Massimo thinks, as he rounds the front of the tanker. "Massimo Venuti," he says, extending a hand down to Davo. "Pleased to meet you."

Davo's shake is strong as he responds, "Gidday, Massimo. Davo. Eddie inside?"

"No, no," Massimo mutters.

Davo grins at Massimo as Pink wheels him through the demolished front wall. "So, you're... looking after the place?" he asks, scrubbing at his beard and making eyes at Pink like Massimo's mad.

Massimo pauses, wondering if he has, in fact, gone mad in this forgotten place where truly anything is possible.

"Must be the new owner," Davo whispers over his shoulder to Pink, since the place is empty and demolition has started.

Massimo stares at Davo, not adverse to that idea.

"What's the matter, Luv?" Pink asks. "Got enough water to make us a cuppa?"

Davo wheels up to the mural, almost running into stark naked Ray in his footy scarf and then all the lights go out.

"Easily fixed," Davo tells Massimo, circling back in his wheelchair. "Give us a hand to rig up the genny."

Pink goes to push Davo's wheelchair, but pulls back, watching with satisfaction how enthusiastically Davo wheels himself outside to do blokey stuff with Massimo.

"Artist, are ya?" Davo ventures. "What's Ray had to say about the liberties you've taken with his *corpus delecti*?" he asks with a grin.

"*Me*? No, I, I am not an artist," Massimo rushes to reply, but Davo interjects with a wink.

"It's a good likeness, mate," Davo assures him. "Although I can't vouch for certain parts that I've never seen before."

*

The generator chugs steadily outside as they sip tea. Pink and Massimo sit on the servery bench with Pink's legs dangling and Massimo's feet on the floor, opposite Davo's wheelchair.

Talking with them has prompted Massimo to confess his feelings for Pearl.

"It was exactly as Mamma said," he relates, sighing sadly. "The right one came out when I forgot where to look, but she wasn't looking for me."

He puts down his empty mug and hugs his lantern to his chest.

"She was here, but where is she now? I cannot go back to *Italia* wondering if she is alright, lost and alone in the bush with a cut foot. I would have driven her, but she refused."

"She's just gone walk-a-bout," Davo says. "She'll be back. Don't worry."

"You are sure?"

"Hundred percent," Davo assures him.

"You picked a hard one with Pearl," Pink puts in. "She's special, alright. If it wasn't for her, I'd still be driving around in a cloud of pink."

She reaches over to ruffle Davo's hair.

"... instead of realising how much I love this big hunk, whichever way he comes."

"Ah, life," Massimo sighs.

He puts down the lantern, pulls out his wallet and hands Pink a credit card.

"I have to go. Please use this to repair the damage I did to the front wall and then cut it up. I thought I could do it, but I cannot say goodbye to her again."

Pink touches his arm reassuringly, "When people say their heart is broken, it means broken open, ready to love properly when the right one comes. You'll see."

"*Si, certo*," Massimo mumbles, with more conviction than he feels, since he will soon be back in *Italia* facing the wrath of Cassandra.

"Love just is," he sighs. "*Perla* didn't need to love me back. But it would have been wonderful."

Massimo shakes Davo's hand, kisses Pink on each cheek, takes a last lingering look at the mural, picks up his keys and lantern and leaves.

*

Pearl is sitting on the edge of the pink bathtub unwinding the now dirty t-towel off her sore foot. She takes off the heirloom necklace and breaks the twine holding the pieces together with her teeth. Slowly, methodically, she scatters the mother-of-pearl pieces in the pink bathtub. She looks at them gleaming white through the sunlit sea water for a long time, stands and strips down to her white bra and knickers. Pensively, she sits on the bath's edge again, listening to the waves crashing against the cliffs far below, worried about what this vision might bring. She swings her legs into the bath and slides under, submerging with an enormous intake of air, utterly surrendering to the spirit of Great-Grandma Pearl.

In her wet, white underwear, Pearl emerges in a shimmering heat haze. Her feet are soon coated with the red dirt of the Kimberley. Her half-dressed, dehydrated great-grandma shuffles toward her painfully slowly. She's as young as Pearl but looks old because she's wafer thin, and her burned, dark skin is flaking off, parchment dry. She holds her dried up water basket before her with a few bush berries in the bottom and the shark tooth in the centre, pointing straight ahead. The red dirt path rises and becomes rocky. Exhausted, Great-Grandma Pearl keeps moving, climbing laboriously in mosquito-ridden humidity over the hot red rocks.

Pearl rushes up, desperate to help, but her ancestor just keeps climbing like she will go straight through her if Pearl gets in the way.

Pearl climbs beside her, waving her arms, softly calling, "I'm here. Your great-granddaughter, Pearl. Can you hear me, Pearl?"

Great-Grandma looks across. Her black eyes flicker with the reflection of Pearl's waving arms, but she doesn't acknowledge this pale girl she sees beside her, who is speaking in a language that she cannot understand. She asks herself: What is Pearl?

As she climbs, Great-Grandma Pearl wonders why she felt so compelled to paint over the sacred hand paintings to show this pale girl that she saw her jumping off these cliffs. She wonders… has she caused all my suffering? Has she returned to see how my suffering ends? Is she a spirit sent to save me?

That's what she believed when she painted her in the cave, but now Great-Grandma Pearl is too exhausted to reach out to see if her eyes are playing tricks. She just keeps moving, a dead woman climbing.

Discouraged, Pearl drops back and trails behind, trying to stay calm about running out of air by painting her ancestor climbing over these red rocks in her mind's eye. She considers breaking the vision, but faintly hears waves crashing against the cliffs below.

Cliffs here?

Great-Grandma Pearl has reached the edge of this world, the Gantheaume Point cliffs, near Broome. Without hesitation, she makes a fist around the shark tooth, discards her water basket and drops off the rugged, red cliffs into the turquoise sea.

"*Noooooooo!*" Pearl yells, scrambling over the rocks, rushing to catch up.

She reaches the edge and leaps off the cliffs into the ocean after her ancestor, yelling, "*HAAAAAaaaahhhh!*"

Desperately short of air, Pearl scans underwater for her ancestor and sees her, clinging with one hand to a rocky outcrop well below the surface, looking petrified.

As Pearl bird-frogs down hard to get to her, a Bronze Whaler makes a lazy turn in their direction. Great-Grandma Pearl stares at it but doesn't flinch. Her free hand remains clenched in a fist around the shark tooth.

Pearl startles as the shark approaches and kicks harder, faster, through sunbeams and a school of silver anchovies swimming fast toward her. Pearl swims straight into her ancestor, who's pressed hard against the rocky outcrop. Willing herself to stay inside her, Pearl bird-frogs them both up as one, surrounded by hundreds of fast circling, dazzling anchovies, up, up to break the surface beside the white hull of a passing pearl lugger.

Pearl passes through her ancestor and emerges in the turquoise sea beside her, screaming, "Here! She's here!" but the Pearler smoking on the deck cannot see or hear her.

Pearl stops yelling, defeated by the sudden realisation that the only ones who ever saw or heard her in visions were the females in her blood line. She looks at Great-Grandma Pearl sinking beneath the surface beside her and her ancestor looks back, mirroring her defeat.

But then the Pearler spots the shark fin surfacing and drops his cheroot as he sees Great-Grandma Pearl sinking in its path. He scrambles down the diver's ladder, leaning way out to reach for her, but the lugger is moving and the shark fast approaching.

Pearl swims back inside her ancestor. Frantically kicking to keep her afloat, Pearl extends her great-grandma's hand above the surface just in time. The Pearler grasps it and pulls Great-Grandma Pearl into his arms, into the love that surely awaits her.

Pearl breaks free and hurtles up into the sitting position, in the pink bathtub on the edge of the world. Gasping for air and crying with relief, she heaves her curly hair back, casting droplets through the cloudless desert sky and puts her face in her hands, struggling to comprehend what just happened.

By the time her breathing settles, Pearl knows what she was put on the Earth to do. Like the pieces of necklace that she collects from the bottom of the pink bathtub, she pieces her visions together.

Gradually, she makes the connection that if she hadn't gone back to save her great-grandma, none of them would have been born, including herself. But, if her great-grandma hadn't seen her jumping off those cliffs, then she never would have painted it and gotten cursed and banished in the first place… So 'seeing' has been their downfall and their saviour.

But 'seeing' has and always will connect them and it's *good* to feel connected, isn't it?

Even dead, Great-Grandma Pearl swam through her to save her from that shark back in Perth, as soon as Pearl jumped in, and now Pearl's saved *her* by doing the same.

Still, it dogs her. Has she inherited a gift or her great-grandma's never-ending trauma? What would her life be like without it?

Flying blind like Mum and Aunty and poor Nana Raeleen? Nup. No way. Not going there.

The more Pearl sees, the more she wants to see. They've always been linked by seeing, destined to protect each other, and knowing that fills the hollowness in her heart.

She wants to yell to her great-grandma, in a way she'll understand, that it's *not* a curse to see. It's what connects them to each other and to other people who might need their help.

Did Great-Grandma know what to do with her gift of seeing, or not?

Pearl reminds herself that she hasn't fully worked out what to do with it, either...

She steps out of the bath and pushes the pieces of necklace into the back pocket of her discarded jeans, where she finds Eddie's nugget...

Pearl pulls out that nugget, takes a long look at it, fuming at the unfairness of Eddie always thinking that she had her head in the water with it when she never bloody well did.

Well, maybe I should now?

Maybe she'll find her dad alive since it was his nugget? *He's* never come back from the dead to make contact. Pearl snap-decides to try, drops the nugget into the bath, impulsively sucks in another huge lungful of air and re-submerges...

Again, she finds herself on a tank stand on the dust-dry Nullarbor Plain looking down, hoping to find her dad alive, but he isn't.

Eddie is kneeling before him, and Pearl pulls back, unable to witness the theft of the nugget again, but this time Eddie is wearing a black shirt.

"Sorry I stole from you," Eddie says to the bag of bones in Big Red's clothes. "Was that what you wanted? Me to give it to her? Well, you got your wish, eh? Fat lot of good it did, since she didn't choose me." He kneels, removes his own hat, which he holds to his chest, adding, "She's gifted, amazing. One in a million. I hope you're proud of her. Rest in peace."

Eddie picks up a shovel from beside his tools, digs it deep into the dry soil beside Big Red's skeleton and pushes it down hard with his steel-capped work boot.

Pearl rises out of the vision and, for the first time in a long time, smiles.

*

Massimo proudly takes Pearl's two paintings off the wall of the monstrosity roadhouse. Ian, the weedy proprietor, stares at the piece of paper in his hand.

"Tempted as I am to not say a word, mate," he says, "but there's too many zeroes on here. The price is three hundred, not thirty grand."

"Under twenty thousand in *Italia*," Massimo replies, "and worth every euro. Please sign for your five percent, pending the co-signature of the artist when she receives the balance."

"Anything you say," Ian replies, signing with a greedy grin.

*

Ray sees Pearl walking back as they wheel in trolleys carrying a couple of kerosene fridges through what was once the front wall of the roadhouse.

"She's baaaack," Ray tells Norm.

Pearl approaches, walking taller and more calmly than they have ever seen before, with no tea-towel around her foot.

"Where've you been?" Ray asks.

"What happened to the front wall?" Norm asks.

"At the cliffs," Pearl replies. "I wanted to see what the front would look like all in glass. Massimo helped."

Ray steps back to better take in the idea of a glass front on the roadhouse.

"Check it out, Norm. Would look bloody good, except for me butt naked in the middle of it," he says for Norm's sake, since Ray always loved being 'out', back in his Melbourne heyday.

Norm rolls his eyes, "Big job."

"You heard Eddie's gone back to work up the line?" Ray asks Pearl, glancing at Norm.

Pearl nods, replying, "Yeah, he's off fixing a few things that he should have fixed a while back."

"Where's the fish tank?" Ray asks.

"Eddie smashed it."

"Curly?"

"Dead."

"Massimo?"

"Gone."

Ray tsks, a bit put out, "Didn't even say goodbye."

"Get over it," Norm growls with a grin.

"You only have to turn your back for a minute 'round here," Ray says as he places his fridge in the dining room where the drinks fridge was.

"Reckon," Norm agrees, as he pushes his fridge into the kitchen.

Noticing the light bulb no longer flickering, Pearl asks, "Thought the generator was on its way out?"

Norm smiles at Ray and says, "Things have a way of coming good, eh, mate?"

"Too right," Ray agrees.

Pearl pulls the last ten litre tin of blue paint over to the Norm and Ray section of the mural and pries it open with a screwdriver. She dips a big brush into what's left and swirls it, ready to start painting over them.

"Onya, Luv," Ray says for Norm's sake, which doesn't stop him whipping out his phone to take photos of them, especially himself painted in all his glory. "Bad day, that."

"Best forgotten," Norm agrees, amused by reprobate Ray pocketing the evidence in his phone.

*

Ray cracks open three cans of Norm's beer from the fridge and takes one to Pearl at the mural.

"You reckon the curse is gone for good now?" he asks.

Pearl takes a sip, wondering how to best try and explain it. "Dunno much about curses," she begins, "but Great-Grandma Pearl got kicked out for painting what she saw on the cave wall over the ancient hand paintings."

Norm and Ray nod, understanding how anyone would get in trouble for that.

"What she saw was me jumping off a cliff," Pearl continues.

Their faces go blank. Both hold their beers in mid-air.

"How could she?" Ray starts, unsure of how to continue. "You weren't even born."

Pearl spreads her hands and shrugs, picking up a brush.

Norm frowns, confused.

Ray goes over and jumps to sit beside him on the servery to watch their mural selves get painted out.

"Nobody likes stuff getting painted about them without their permission," Pearl begins, laying the brush on the upturned lid. "I'm really sorry I did that to you," she adds, sincerely looking across at Norm, who nods, appreciating her saying that. "But I'm glad Great-Grandma painted me jumping off a cliff," Pearl shares, "because she needed to show me something about us that she didn't understand, even if it got her in big trouble."

After a long pause, Norm puts his beer can on the servery and goes over to Pearl. "There's something that needs to be said, and I'm gunna say it," he begins. "Seeing stuff about everyone 'round here in the fish tank was weird, no two ways about it, but what you saw was spot on every time, even if none of us wanted to face it. You're special, Pearl. Pink says so, Massimo said so, and we say so."

"More than just special, Norman – she's a *healer*," Ray insists, jumping down to join them. "You've given Norm and me a lot to talk about," he says, about to elaborate, but Norm gives him a forbidding look.

Ray shrugs and retorts, "We're all pages written on, Norman."

Pearl doesn't know what to say as this new connected feeling inside her intensifies, a warm enveloping feeling that she imagines feels something like… love.

Norm sees it in her gaze, a softening of the dark tension that was always lurking there.

"You should keep using it to help people," he reckons.

Pearl shrugs, "Dunno if I'd call it helping."

Ray continues, "Like this Japanese cyclist, Juno, we've got staying at Country Downs. Been pedalling his legs off across the desert looking for answers and not finding any. Doesn't say much. Needs all the inspiration he can get. Could you give him a hand?"

Pearl casts a hand at the bare globe hanging from the ceiling, "Haven't got a fish tank. Or a fish."

"Easily fixed," Ray responds. "People will come," he says, with a dreamy wave at the sky. "I'll do a mail drop, Pearl's Place: an oasis of spiritual guidance in the desert. It doesn't have to be a petrol station anymore, Luv – I mean Pearl. The world's full of walking woundeds."

Pearl's quiet, not convinced that staying on here would be the right thing to do, even if she could. "Have you two forgotten that we're getting kicked out on the tenth?" she reminds them.

"We could set it up at our place," Ray suggests.

"Perfect part of the Country Downs experience," Norm adds.

Pearl shakes her head. "Nah. Gunna bury Dad and make up with Mum, but you could ask Aunty. She could… maybe."

Ray looks at Norm, "Oh, really?"

"Even with?" Norm asks, holding a hand over his right eye.

Pearl nods, still finding it hard to believe that she'll have to find her dad's remains without Eddie, especially after hearing those nice words he said about her to Red's skeleton. Misunderstandings, so many bloody misunderstandings.

She is about to ask Norm which way Eddie went when Ian, the monstrosity proprietor, pulls up outside, distracting her as he enters. He walks directly to Pearl with a thick manila envelope and hands it to her.

"What's this for?" she asks, peering into the envelope, shocked.

"Some Italian loonie came in," Ian says, "insisting on paying too much for your paintings."

"Massimo!" the trio say in unison.

"That's him," Ian answers, proffering Pearl a pen and a piece of paper, "Sign here."

Pearl cannot believe the amount on the page, "Thirty thousand dollars!"

"Twenty-eight five, after commission," Ian advises, pointing to the appropriate clause.

Gob-smacked, Pearl signs and hands him back his paper and pen.

"Ta," Ian says as he heads out.

"Wait!" Pearl calls, racing after him. "Give us a lift. I've got to call Aunty!"

Chapter Fifteen

Pearl feels insanely happy, having sent most of Massimo's money straight to Aunty's bank account, just in time to get the debt collectors off their backs. She almost floats back to the roadhouse, even though she's full of fast food and carrying groceries.

Relieved to see that Norm and Ray have gone, Pearl puts away the groceries with her mind on the mural. How fantastic, she thinks, to be given this time to paint all day and sleep all night; or paint in her sleep, without worrying about getting kicked out. And she's not going to bed hungry anymore either, thanks to Massimo.

Thank you so much. Sorry I couldn't love you the way you wanted me to, Massimo. Glad you liked my paintings.

Pearl stands before her mural gazing at it, not quite meditating, but close. Until now, someone was always on her, telling her off, like her experiences were not hers to paint. And this silence, except for the birds outside twittering and swearing at each other, is so soothing. She feels like an uncaged bird, thanks to Massimo banging down that front wall. A pair of fearless Willy Wagtails hop in, wagging their tails and firing off machine gun chatter at her, which snaps Pearl out of her creative gaze with a smile.

Meditating. As if.

She walks outside and crosses the highway to sit on her hillock, liking the way the orange sunset softens the sledge-hammered front of the roadhouse. Being this far away makes it easy to see the big gaps in the mural that she can now fill, peacefully in her own time.

The Wedge-tailed Eagle that amazed her on her way back here to her birthplace reappears. It breaks Pearl's vision of the mural, swooping before her like a reminder and then sharply rises, majestically outlined by the setting sun.

It tilts its head down to look directly at Pearl and sends out a stark call that's more like a shriek, as if trying to wake her up to something she should already know.

Astonished, Pearl thinks: rise above.

The eagle flaps its enormous wings once to cross the highway and effortlessly glides over the roadhouse.

Okay, got that. Be an eagle and rise… Like how?

By not getting angry or snooty, or worse, abandoning family like they abandoned me. By not charading and keeping shameful secrets. Learned that from everyone, especially them…

By loving her messed up family, because that's where she came from, and by paying them respect with the gift of seeing that she's been given… Pearl doesn't know where that came from, maybe the eagle, but it feels right, so right. Her heart warms to it as her new way forward… She decides to just paint this mural from her heart, from the beginning to the end of her short, weird life so far. And she further decides that she's not going to paint anyone else's story but her family's, because other people's stories are not hers to tell.

Pearl heads back to the mural, mixes some paint and begins all the way to the left, with Marnie's round mouth, like a donut of chain-smoking derision. Having made a good start, she heads for bed, dying to catch up on all the sleep that she didn't get while out in the bush.

*

When Pearl wakes beneath the mural, she shuffles back on her bum, pleased that she has added the rest of Marnie in her sleep. Hands on hips, Marnie's glaring at Red and young Pearl painted on the caravan park fence. Not bad, Pearl admits to herself.

And so, the competition begins…

Pearl sets to work trying to out-paint her night's work, by adding her furious-self jumping off the caravan park cliff, almost into the jaws of the Bronze Whaler. Below the surface, the eerie, almost see-through spirit of Great-Grandma Pearl waits in a cave to save her.

Water.

Water-the-conductor is the perfect link between these visions, Pearl thinks. Water was always there, before conception, before man, when everything was aqueous and unformed. She pensively swishes her brush through the blue-tinged water in what was once Curly's jar and begins to blend in the transitions, gazing at this water like it's the womb of the world. Something needs to go into the space before the Nullarbor cave part of the mural and Pearl knows that water will give it life in this desert place. Enlivening the paints that she mixes, Pearl surrenders to water the conductor and feels born again.

*

Days and nights blend into each other like the colours Pearl mixes as the story emerges chronologically. Again, she paints baby Beryl's alarm at seeing Pearl in the fish tank with her, while dragging startled young Marnie's face beneath the surface by the heirloom necklace.

Pearl paints on without noticing when she pauses to drink, eat, or snatch a few hours of sleep. There is only the work and the occasional shower.

*

Pearl emerges from the shower one morning realising that she needs to add some hand paintings to the Nullarbor cave section. She lightens the lines of her already-painted-self jumping off the cliffs on the cave wall that Great-Grandma Pearl painted and adds hints of the hands beneath. Now it's perfect. The angry elder's arm is perfectly flung out, banishing her devastated ancestor with his shark tooth falling into her water basket. But something is missing, a dot of doubt in the elder's eye, which Pearl adds because she saw it.

Eddie stealing the nugget from her dead dad is already painted in next. Pearl decides that it has to stay because her dad was family, never mind about Eddie. She begins to paint her horrified self looking down on this from high on the tank stand when a van pulls up outside, blocking her light.

Pearl shudders as she turns and reads Kalgoorlie Specialty Markets on the side.

Vince and Doof jump down, open the back and begin wheeling in the square Formica tables and red vinyl chairs that they took, piling them into an untidy mess in the dining room.

Pearl paints on, ignoring them as they put the fridges and freezer back next to Norm and Ray's kerosene ones. She's too engrossed in her work to care what they're saying to each other. It's just as Norm said: things have a way of coming good.

"Sign here," Vince tells her, shoving a printed inventory page under her nose and a pen, ruining her focus.

Pearl glances at the servery.

"Cash register," she replies, matching his condescending gaze until he looks away.

Smoke-stinky Vince juts his chin at Doof, who goes out to the van to retrieve it.

Pearl reads the inventory of returned goods and signs, handing it back to Vince as Doof wheels in the cash register.

"Don't leave it empty," she tells Vince as she turns her back on him and returns to her work. "That Coke you stole needs paying for."

She smiles to herself as she hears him chuck a coin in the cash register and slam it, proud that they can no longer intimidate her.

As they wheel their empty trolleys out, she calls over her shoulder, "Bye, boys."

Relieved to hear them driving off, Pearl puts down her paint brush and stretches her aching shoulders by hanging off the servery door frame.

She grabs a stale chicken roll from Norm's fridge in the kitchen and sits on one of the returned chairs to eat it. She's too tired to imagine in detail what goes next in the mural, so she decides to leave it to her sleeping-self. Pearl finishes her roll, puts the chairs and tables back where they used to be and heads for bed early.

*

In the morning, she's pleased to see herself in the mural, sitting on the side of the pink bathtub, unwinding the bandage off her foot on the edge of the world. She likes that she left the finale of her jumping off the cliffs after her great-grandma to be painted by light of day.

And what a glorious day it is. Now that summer's passing, a cooler breeze is flowing through the dining room. Emaciated, young Great-Grandma Pearl is dropping off the red rocky cliffs clutching her shark tooth. It takes Pearl the whole day to get that right, because she still feels haunted by what would have happened if she hadn't jumped in after her... But jump in she did, above her ailing ancestor, who's dropping like a stone, half in and half out of the water, with Pearl yelling, leaping off the rocks above her.

Pearl doesn't even attempt to sleep as she paints the Bronze Whaler lurking below and the pearl lugger nearly passing. In the next section, Pearl paints herself emerging out of her ancestor as Peter Pearler pulls Great-Grandma Pearl to his chest.

Painting that part of the mural brings up emotions buried deep within Pearl. Warm tears sting her eyes. She cries with relief because she was able to save her great-grandma. She cries even harder because, despite the worst of the worst things happening to her, Great-Grandma Pearl ended up in the arms of someone who'd love her and give her a baby to love in the time she had left to live.

Even if he was married.

She wanders to bed wiping away her tears with her paint-splattered shirt sleeve, willing her sleeping-self to paint her great-grandma's demise, because it's too gruesome to face awake.

*

And paint it in her sleep, she does. Pearl wakes at the base of the mural with blood red paint on her hands, dreading to look up and see the detail.

Her ancestor's panicked face is submerging in a sea of red with her waist ripped open by the monster's sawing jaws. On deck, little Raeleen's screaming her lungs out, wearing her mother's necklace, safe in the devastated pearler's arms. The panicked deckhands lurch the lugger toward Pearl's doomed ancestor, with their useless boat hooks extended…

Pearl looks away.

Aunty was right. Sometimes, it's a terrible thing to see.

She backs away, glaring left at the elder who's throwing his hateful shark tooth at Great-Grandma Pearl, sealing her fate.

Pink and Davo slowly pull up outside, but Pearl barely notices them, or the enormous, blanket-wrapped sheets of glass strapped to the sides of the water tanker. Norm and Ray pull in behind them as Pearl heads into the kitchen to wash the red paint off her hands.

Norm and Ray halt in the ragged entrance.

"Wow," Norm says, gaping at the enormity of the mural.

"You alright?" Ray asks ratty-haired Pearl, who's looking sombrely at them from the kitchen.

Pearl gives him a distracted nod as she enters, wiping her hands on a t-towel. She knows her overalls are paint-splattered and her hair's out of control, but she's beyond caring.

The mural is all that matters now.

Pink wheels Davo inside in his wheelchair, suddenly halting at the sight of the mural.

Davo lets out an impressed whistle. "I thought it looked good before," he tells Pink, "but this is a bloody masterpiece."

Pink walks over to Pearl saying, "I owe you an apology, Luv, for spitting the dummy about my bracelet."

"The name's Pearl. Apology accepted. Good to see you, Pink."

"The name's Pat," Pink replies, holding Pearl's gaze. "Haven't been Pink since you sorted my head out. And my wardrobe."

Pearl smiles, taking in Pat's non-pink outfit as she wheels Davo over to meet her.

"This is Davo, my true love," Pat says. "Although it's not the first time you've seen him. We've come to put in the glass front that Massimo paid for."

Pearl frowns, wondering why he did that. Buying her paintings was enough.

"He felt bad about wrecking the place," Pat begins.

Davo interjects, "So we let him pay for the glass and these louts volunteered to put it in," he adds, smiling at Norm and Ray, who don't hear him.

They're slowly making their way along the mural, engrossed in the details. A slightly built Japanese man wanders in through the entrance and stops, also amazed by the mural.

"Who's this?" Norm turns to ask Pearl, pointing to the dead man that Eddie is stealing the nugget from.

"Tell ya later," she replies, as she notices the man lingering in the entrance, feeling like she's seen him somewhere before.

"And who's this?" she asks them.

"Juno," Ray replies. "Our first County Downs guest. Well, sort of a guest. We picked him up off the side of the road. Bit hard to ask him to give us a hand, since he doesn't speak English, but he looks fit enough."

"Did his bike have saddle bags over the sides?" she asks, suddenly remembering seeing a Japanese rider out of the bus window at Coolgardie.

"Sure did," Ray says.

Must've taken him all this time, Pearl thinks, incredulously.

Recognising her as the artist, Juno gives Pearl a reverent little bow.

Pat boils the kettle as Norm, Ray and Juno head out to unload something off the back of Norm's truck. They stagger in, all wearing thick welding gloves, carrying another fish tank, which they place on the floor next to the big, old TV stand where the last one was. They look at Pearl, hoping that she'll like it, but she's not liking the idea of putting her head in a fish tank again. Not without Curly.

"Don't fill it up," she tells Norm and Ray as the trio move the TV stand to the servery wall and reposition the fish tank in the middle of the room where the TV stand was.

As Norm and Ray head out and return with an old TV with a rabbit ears aerial and place it on the stand, Juno leans into the empty tank. He pulls off his necklace with a tiny gold pagoda pendant dangling off it and places it in the bottom of the tank, like Ray showed him at County Downs.

Pearl gives Ray a look, "Did you put him up to that?"

"Tide's out," Ray replies, giving her his cheekiest grin. "Any man who rides across the Nullarbor on a pushbike in summer needs *guidance.*"

Pearl resists a smile as she goes through to help Pat bring out the teas and coffees.

As the glass is positioned into aluminium frames, the trio of men grunt with exertion behind Pearl, whose only focus is finishing off the mural. Occasionally she hears Pat and Davo yelling instructions, but mostly she just zones out.

In the mural, Eddie emerges in his black shirt on one knee with his hat to his chest, belatedly paying his respects to Red's skeleton in baggy clothes. Painted Pearl rises from the pink bathtub at the end, gasping and gazing back at it all.

In the mural, as in life, she is paying her respects to all of her family who have gone before, secretly hoping to find her dad's remains soon.

*

When she is finished painting, Pearl takes a few courageous steps back to take it all in, utterly exhausted, but satisfied. What a day it's been. What a summer. She looks around, wondering where everyone has gone. She takes in the glass front of the roadhouse for the first time, switches on the light above the empty tank and heads outside to see it from her hillock.

It's just as she imagined. The roadhouse looks like a giant

fish tank in the desert when the mural's lit up at night. She decides to fill up the new tank tomorrow to enhance the effect.

Doesn't mean I have to stick my head in it.

Chuffed, Pearl hugs her knees as she sits, feeling fully integrated with as much of the story that she knows. Having painted the past and given it to the roadhouse, she feels like it's completed... and she likes not being able to see any further ahead than that. The only things that ever hold her are things that are unresolved, mysteries that are unsolved... like what it would be like to go all the way with Eddie. Pearl thinks kindly of him as she heads back, remembering the nice things he said about her being gifted and amazing to Big Red's skeleton.

She holds the thought about going all the way with Eddie as she enters the roadhouse, and the longer she holds it the better it feels, which surprises her. Gone are all her usual evasions and reservations because love isn't the fear of not knowing what to do, or of being abandoned, is it? No, her new-self answers. The only snag is that she still doesn't know where to find him. But then she remembers what Eddie's said, soon after they met, while he was walking away with his windmill blade glinting in the rising sun...

Energised, she rushes into the kitchen, grabs a torch and Yanush's steel meat tenderising mallet and races outside. She clambers up on to the windmill platform with the mallet in the bib of her overalls and a torch in her mouth, wondering how hard it could be to break off some bolts and stash a windmill blade under the caravan. How long would it take for the bush telegraph to tell Eddie that a blade's missing off Aunty's windmill? Pearl raises the mallet, hoping that she won't go the way of Big Red before Eddie finds out, but then stops.

She still needs the windmill to fill up the fish tank.

Madness!

She sighs, hoping that the bush telegraph at least told Eddie that she rejected Massimo before he went back to Italy alone. That is, if Eddie's still interested in her, at all.

She hears a ute pulling in, sees its headlights and hastily switches off the torch.

Talk about being careful what you wish for!

Pearl turns, but it's not Eddie's ute, even though its diesel engine growls the same.

She's surprised to see a fit, young blackfella jumping out of the old ute in a Dockers hoodie, jeans and runners. Pearl stays on the windmill platform, waiting to see what he wants. He cups his hands on the glass and peers through, side-stepping along to take in the mural.

"Pearl," he calls through the fly strips.

Pearl startles. How does he know my name?

"It's Marlon."

Marlon?

"Youngy when I was little."

That name brings up memories as she quietly climbs down. My little playmate, Youngy?

"Over here," she says as she approaches Marlon in the light.

Marlon spins 'round and takes her in, dazzling her with a huge grin.

"Long time, no see, Pearl." Then he pushes the hoodie off his head and points. "Deadly art. Did you paint that?"

Pearl nods and beams, happy to finally see a blackfella that she used to know, especially one with a killer smile and cute ponytail. She pulls the plastic strips aside to let him in.

"Yeah, I painted it," she says, once they are inside. "Where you been? Nobody hangs around here anymore. Aunty says everyone went to the city. So did I, remember? Mum and Dad took me to school in Perth when I was six."

"*Unna*," Marlon mutters, remembering the wrench of that parting only too well. They were solid little besties, even though her mum never liked him and always acted white.

He looks at Pearl and decides to put into practice something Uncle Charlie has been on at him to do every single day: just say what's true as.

"Dunno 'bout everyone, but I went to Perth and ran amuck;

sniffin', boozing', dope, trying to fill up something that felt empty inside. It's different in the city. Too much shame. Came back here to country with Uncle Charlie so he could sort my head out," he admits with a grin, "so lock up ya petrol and piss, sis!" he adds, grinning wider.

Pearl can't resist a smile, even though she's not quite sure how to read him. She feels strangely similar to him, comfortable with his directness. "Where's your Uncle?"

"Camped out near the big place up the road where we filled up the ute. He's fast asleep under the stars by now. It's the only time he ever stops yakking."

Love it.

"When we were driving past that old fridge door out the front with 'Closed and For Immediate Sale' painted on it, I remembered playing chasey with you 'round here," Marlon adds. "Came back and saw the lights on so I thought I'd drop in just in case you were here. Didn't expect this though," he adds, gesturing with wide arms at the mural.

"Yeah, well we're all out of petrol and piss," Pearl replies, returning his cheeky grin. "And I don't smoke dope, so that mural will have to do, unless you want a cuppa?"

"Nah," Marlon replies, liking her giving him lip as he goes over to check out the mural.

And then he sees the Nullarbor cave section. Marlon stands before it, feeling nothing short of astonished.

"I *know* this story," he whispers, turning to Pearl. "Uncle Charlie's been telling me about it like what happens when a man gets out of control and does stuff he'll regret for the rest of his life. Like Great-Grandpa, Joe, there," he says, pointing to the elder in the mural.

Equally astonished, Pearl also points, saying, "That's my great-grandma he's telling off."

"I know," Marlon answers sadly. "Ruined his life."

"Didn't do her any favours, either," Pearl replies, hands on her hips.

Marlon takes in what happened next in the mural and responds, "Glad she didn't die. Is that you jumping in after her? Did you dream that, Pearl?"

Pearl nods, feeling a bit tight-lipped, not ready to explain about all the women in her line seeing stuff in water.

She grimly points further on to the shark attack, saying, "She didn't die right away, but he threw that shark tooth at her."

Marlon sees the shark attack and the pain in Pearl's hazel eyes, the dark shadows lurking there, so like his own. He'd be prepared to bet that she wouldn't come easy back to culture because of what happened in that cave. And he'd like to help, but he's torn because she needs to understand it from the female elders, not from him.

"Uncle Charlie's *got* to see this," he says, pointing at the cave section. "I'll bring him tomorrow."

He pulls his keys out of the back pocket of his jeans, but Pearl reaches out and touches his arm, asking, "What does he say about it again?"

Marlon sighs and decides to tell her some, not all, or he'll be the one in big trouble.

"He reckons Great-Grandpa Joe got in big trouble with the women for doing that," he adds. "They jarred him, gave him a hiding with their sticks, but that didn't stop it ruining his life, thinking that he'd sent her to her death. She didn't know that he was just trying to tell her off for painting over those hand paintings."

"Me," Pearl interrupts. "She painted me, jumping off a cliff."

Not understanding, Marlon nods and continues, "He was trying to scare her out of jumping off The Bight with that shark tooth of his," he adds, "because shark was his totem. Probably all he could think of 'cause he was wild, but later on he was so sorry he did that. He never stopped looking for her."

Pearl is too confronted by this new understanding of the bastard elder she saw and painted that she doesn't know how to answer.

"Does nobody no good going against lore," Marlon adds,

heading out.

"What'ya mean, law?"

Marlon knows when to shut up. Only the women can tell her that.

Pearl's head's spinning. Could what his Uncle Charlie says about the elder be true? If it is, then it was the most tragic misunderstanding for both of them and everyone in their families ever since.

Marlon sees her struggling and feels sorry that he can't say more. He takes her chin in his hand and looks into her eyes, saying, "It's not that someone got hurt, but that everyone did."

Tears well up in Pearl because she still feels partially responsible for that.

Marlon lets go and heads out to his ute, calling behind him, "See you tomorrow, sis."

Pearl watches him go, longing to know more, but needing some space to think about how wrong they all might have been, starting with the elder and Great-Grandma Pearl.

Marlon calls behind him, "Uncle Charlie's a tough old man, so don't let on that you know Joe's story. He'll tell you, if he's gunna. He might be your uncle, too. What's your totem animal, sis?"

"Eagle," Pearl replies before she can even think about it. What do I fuckin' know about totems?

"I'm a *Djitti Djitti*," Marlon says with a grin, "Willy Wagtail – can't you tell?"

He does a couple of footy ducks and weaves to amuse her before he jumps into the ute.

"I'm always rushing 'round, being a messenger and defending my mob. Some women of the shark dreaming will come," he calls out of the ute window, "once Uncle Charlie sees the mural. They'll fill you in about that shark," he adds, jutting his chin at the Tiger Shark in the mural. "Then you won't have so many holes of your own to fill up, Pearl. I promise."

Totally hooked on solving this new mystery, Pearl watches Marlon's headlights growing smaller on the highway as he heads toward the monstrosity. She turns back to the mural and takes a long hard look at the Nullarbor cave section, especially the dot of doubt that she added to the elder's eye.

Chapter Sixteen

Pearl sleeps soundly for the first time in ages and is pleased to wake in her bed feeling refreshed. She lies in for a while, considering what she learned from Marlon yesterday. She hopes he will bring his uncle today, as promised, to help her unravel the mystery. The only word she remembers from her cave vision was *marbun*, said by her great-grandma to the elder. If Aunty's right, *marbun* means curse. Was she asking if he was cursing her? Maybe Great-Grandma Pearl was threatening *him*? She was the seer, and he was out of line telling her off, especially if he got a hiding over it from the other women.

She sits bolt upright in bed.

What if *she* cursed him?

Ridiculous.

Pearl reminds herself that she didn't see that. She saw her devastated ancestor accepting her fate, but, if it also ruined his life, then he suffered too. None of it is happy making, she thinks, as she heads into the roadhouse to wash her hair. But it is comforting that it may all have been a big misunderstanding. Holding grudges against him hasn't done any of the women in her line any good. And she needs to get to the bottom of it today.

She lets the jets of water massage her eyelids as she goes back over all that she didn't know when she came back here. Her visions have revealed how full of misunderstandings life is and how the learning never ends. How many secrets have been revealed, especially about all the women in her line being seers and not cursed? It sure looked like Marlon's Great-Grandpa Joe didn't know that Great-Grandma Pearl was a seer. Even if he had, how likely would it be that he understood that she was painting her descendent jumping off a cliff in the future?

No chance.

Maybe he felt threatened by her psychic abilities? Or maybe he was flat out trying to teach her a lesson and afraid for her, like Marlon said. Whatever his reasons, painting Pearl is what caused the misunderstanding, so that old feeling of being responsible for everything wrong with the family begins to dog her again. Pearl feels for the taps and turns off the water, determined not to go there.

Rise above, rise above, rise above.

As she waits for Marlon to bring his uncle, Pearl busies herself with washing the piled-up dishes and transferring the food from Norm's kerosene fridge into the old one that came back. She then turns her attention to putting Bubba and Bear's clothes back on hangers in their wardrobe.

*

Just after lunch, Marlon's wiry Uncle Charlie steps barefoot in black jeans down from the driver's side of the ute. His white hair and beard stand out against his Indigenous flag t-shirt.

Pearl comes out to greet them, noticing the kind way he looks at her, sort of into her.

"Gidday, Bub," he says. "Marlon reckons you're a proper artist."

Bub?

That's a bit too close to Bubba for Pearl's liking, but she's not about to correct him. "Hi, Charlie," she replies. "I'm Pearl. Would you like a cup of tea?"

"Yes please," Charlie answers with a smile, revealing a pink tongue like Pearl's and a mouth full of uneven teeth. "Bub, you can call me Uncle."

Pearl doesn't know how to respond to that. Mum and Aunty didn't have any brothers.

"Milk and three sugars for him," Marlon puts in, noticing her discomfort. "Just water for me, thanks."

"Come on in… Uncle," Pearl says, opening the fly strips, which Charlie ducks through.

Marlon hangs back to whisper in her ear, "He calls all the

girls Bub. We all call him Uncle. Don't worry about it."

Pearl nods, raising her eyebrows as she heads in after Charlie, who's already inspecting the cave confrontation in the mural.

He nods to himself, as if he's aware of what happened between his grandad and Pearl's great-grandma from the stories handed down.

Sadly, he peers toward the end, where Pearl's emaciated ancestor drops off the cliffs to her death. What he doesn't understand is why Pearl's painted herself jumping off above her. That makes no sense. He turns to look intensely at Pearl. Why did she paint that? Is she feeling suicidal in solidarity with her ancestor? Charlie has devoted his life to saving troubled kids, and it worries him right away that he may be looking at another one.

The intensity in his gaze halts Pearl on her way to the kitchen to make the tea.

"Who told you these stories and gave you permission to paint them, Bub?" Charlie asks.

"Nobody told me," Pearl mutters, mulishly not wanting to elaborate.

Permission! Charlie probably doesn't get it any more than his Grandpa Joe did.

"If she jumped off those cliffs, she died," Charlie says, from what he knows of the story.

"If she died, I wouldn't be here," Pearl counters, not liking where his assumption's headed.

Charlie takes a long time to consider that the handed down version of the story might not be right. If Pearl's ancestor lived, then all the suffering that his grandpa went through, believing that he had accidentally sent her to her death, was for nothing, poor fella. He looks again at the mural and sees the striking similarity between Pearl and her ancestor, thinking, blow me down, she lived!

Pearl leaves him with it, as she heads into the kitchen to make his tea.

Marlon points to the cave confrontation and urgently asks Charlie, "That's him for sure, isn't it? Great-Grandpa Joe?"

Charlie nods grimly. He had been of a mind to make this lost girl welcome, to invite the Women of the Shark Dreaming to come and share stories with her to bring her back to culture, but she must be honest with him first.

Pearl hands Marlon a glass of water and Charlie his mug of tea, determined to tackle what she needs to know head on. She stands in front of the local cave, facing them.

"You know what she asked him? *Marbun?* Why would she ask him that, Uncle?"

Shocked, Charlie puts down his tea. Marlon looks at her like she just made a major boo-boo.

Gone is the soft spoken 'Bub' as Charlie now demands to know, "I'll ask you again. Who has been telling you these stories and giving you permission to paint them?"

Marlon gulps down his water, worried for her.

"Great-Grandma Pearl," Pearl replies, pointing at her in the cave. "She didn't ask permission to paint me on the cave wall, and he didn't answer her either."

Charlie stares at her, suddenly uneasy. Doesn't she know her great-grandma's real name? And if Kalinda has been appearing to her, he has no business asking her any more about it.

Misreading his silence as disbelief, Pearl blurts out, "She didn't exactly tell me," she begins, casting an arm at the entire mural. "I saw all of this in water. Nobody ever tells me anything, so *why start now?*"

Charlie glances at what else happens in the mural and recoils from the part where Pearl comes out of being inside her ancestor. "I gotta go get the women, Bub," he calls over his shoulder as he bolts through the fly strips, leaving his steaming mug of tea behind.

Charlie urgently beckons for Marlon to move it as he sees him whispering to her, "The women will come. He can't talk to you about women's business."

Pearl pushes the fly strips aside to watch Marlon rounding the ute.

He winks at her over the roof, calling out to Charlie as he

climbs in, "How come every time I meet a pretty girl you tell me we're *related?*"

Charlie flicks Pearl a tense wave goodbye and guns it onto the highway.

Pearl watches them go feeling confused about what she did that was so wrong. She wonders how long these Women of the Shark Dreaming will take to turn up. She imagines them coming in with shark fins strapped to their backs, like kids scare each other with in the surf and instantly dismisses that thought as disrespectful and stupid.

Rules, rules, rules.

Why can't people be just like her, honest, laying stuff out as they see it, like a pancake on a plate? It doesn't feel good not to have a clue about what 'women's business' is, either.

Maybe Aunty knows?

Pearl jogs into the office, picks up the phone and is pleased to hear that the dial tone's back. She dials the number Yanush scribbled on his desk pad for Midland Hospital.

*

Discovering from the hospital that Beryl left with her sister and partner two weeks ago, Pearl faces a difficult decision. To get to Aunty, she will have to go through her mum, and she doesn't relish the thought of that. Marnie may be harsh, she thinks, but a nurse she will always be, so it makes sense that she wanted Aunty and Yanush to stay with her while Aunty got over her operation. And they had no reason to rush back, especially with their debts paid off.

Maybe they don't know the phone's back on, or they would have called, wouldn't they?

They sent no messages via Norm and Ray.

Not happy about feeling invisible, Pearl picks up the phone and puts it down a few times. Her needs still don't matter to the olds, she realises, but they matter to her. She asks herself what she really needs from this phone call: to feel connected, to ask how Aunty is, and to tell them what's been happening ever since the sale of her paintings saved the roadhouse. So, what's stopping her?

Everything is the wrong way 'round, Pearl realises. They're the ones who always withheld the truth about our First Nation's heritage. They're the ones who made me believe that we're cursed because we see stuff in water, and they're the ones who conveniently let me blame that elder, who wasn't blameless, but still… why the hell do I want love from the likes of them?

Because they're family?

Pearl paces a few sweaty laps of the dining room before she returns to the office and dials until it rings out. She doesn't leave a message, feeling almost relieved.

What would they know about women's business anyway?

She slams down the phone and walks out, preferring to wait for the Women of the Shark Dreaming.

*

Pearl's restless sleep-in is broken by the sound of Ray's crop duster, chugging low over the roadhouse. She dashes out and shades her eyes from the sun that is already high in the sky.

The crop duster is towing a 'Welcome Home Bubba, Bear and Marnie' banner behind it and Ray's enthusiastically waving out of the crop duster's window, yelling, "See you tomorra."

Marnie? Fuck!

Pearl dashes around the front in time to see Aunty and Yanush's old sedan pulling in, with them all waving up at Ray… including her mum from the back seat.

As Ray flies back to Country Downs, the gob-smacked trio stare at the gleaming glass front of the roadhouse, revealing their first glimpse of the mural. And then they see Pearl fast approaching, barefoot in her long t-shirt.

Pearl's heart is thumping as she rushes around to Aunty's side to give her a fierce hug before she can even get her seatbelt undone.

Yanush is the first out of the car. "Thought we'd surprise you, kiddo, but you surprised us," he says, indicating the mural.

"It's magnificent," he adds as he stands, legs apart, taking in the glass-fronted roadhouse. "Like a fresco in a fish tank."

Pearl chuckles as she reminds him, "You said it. Paint all you like, kid, as long as it's walls."

Beryl gets out of the car, turning to better see what they're on about with her good eye. Pearl leads her inside by the hand, glancing back at Marnie, who's still wrestling out of her seat belt while trying to light a cigarette.

"Don't know if I can take it all in at once," Beryl begins, stalling with each step as she gazes at Pearl's mural.

Beryl points to her baby-self, in shock from seeing Pearl in the fish tank with her, the day she and Marnie almost drowned.

Marnie joins them to look at it and tells Beryl, "That's exactly what happened, eh, sis?" She turns to Pearl, adding, "I saw you in there, but I didn't know you were you. How could I? My own kid when I was just a little kid myself."

"Terrible thing, being a child that sees," Beryl reminds Pearl, who is more worried about her mum making her way along the mural before she can tell her that Big Red has died.

She sidesteps and pulls Marnie's hand toward her, saying "I'm sorry about what happened back in Perth, Mum."

Marnie's adversarial look zeroes in on her, but Pearl averts her gaze and swiftly moves on. "How are you, Aunty?"

"Quack doctor in Ceduna gave me glaucoma eye drops," Beryl replies, "then they said cancer in Midland, but you know, and I know. Not wanting to see cost me my eye."

Pearl nods, noticing Marnie glancing at the rest of the mural. She moves to obscure her view.

Yanush comes over to put an arm around Beryl, saying, "It's beautiful, that new eye."

Pearl looks closely at Beryl's glass eye and can barely see the difference. "It's perfect. The left eye can still see, Aunty. People will come. They'll want you to see what's holding them back in life. Norm and Ray will bring them."

Beryl and Marnie shake their heads in unison.

"Couldn't do what you do," Beryl says.

"Can't paint to save my life," Marnie puts in.

"You wouldn't have to," Pearl replies. "Just tell 'em what you see."

Beryl looks challenged, almost excited and a little bit scared. "What? In there?" she asks, eyeing the water in the fish tank on the floor. "You know I can't swim."

Pearl nods, smiling, "At least you won't have to climb on a chair."

Beryl looks at Yanush, returning from the car with a bottle of vodka.

"If I needed a glass eye," he tells her, "I'd have to have two. A white one for the night before, and a red one for the morning after."

Beryl gives him a sidelong look and asks, "What if I started seeing out of my good eye, Bear, if people come around looking for help?"

Yanush salutes her with the vodka bottle. "It's your life, Bubba, as long as you don't stop seeing me."

"Can't do it if I don't understand," Beryl tells Pearl, indicating the mural.

Marnie asks, "Why'd you jump in with that shark back home?"

"Was mad enough with you to jump off a cliff," Pearl replies. "Must've been in training, but I didn't know it then."

Pearl pulls up three chairs. "Please sit down," she says. "I've got something sad to tell you."

They sit before Pearl and her work.

Pearl quietly breaks it to them, "Dad's dead."

In the shocked silence, Pearl steps aside so they can take in the rest of the mural. She points at the nugget theft.

Marnie grinds her cigarette out under her white thong, gets up and stares at the skeleton at the base of the windmill that Eddie is stealing the nugget off, asking, "Is that *Red*?"

Pearl nods. "The windmill was busted, and he died of thirst."

"Serves him fuckin' right," Marnie mutters, sloping back to slump in her chair.

"You saw that?" Aunty asks, looking at poor Red in the mural, "all on your own?"

Pearl nods, close to tears.

"You could've drowned!" Marnie snaps, glaring at her.

"Come here," Aunty says, pulling Pearl to sit on her lap for a hug like she used to when Pearl was little. "Poor bugger. No wonder he didn't send money home," Beryl tells Marnie. "You can't get money out of a dead man."

"*He* did," Marnie says, pointing to the guy stealing the nugget.

In the uncomfortable silence that follows, Yanush tells Marnie, "That's Eddie. Good bloke, used to work here."

"Good thief," Marnie mutters.

Pearl points to the end of the mural, saying, "He went back and apologised, when he fixed the windmill."

"Better late than never," Yanush puts in.

"We've got to find Dad," Pearl tells them, "and give him a proper burial."

Aunty hugs her tighter as the trio nod in silent, sombre agreement, still finding it hard to believe that Red has passed away.

*

It takes Beryl and Marnie most of the day to work out all of the threads in the mural, while Yanush brings their bags in, fetches Marnie an ashtray and makes sandwiches, which they eat in the dining room.

Beryl takes another long look at the progression of events in the mural and asks, "This is how it all happened, but then you went back?"

"Yep," Pearl replies, with a mouth full of sandwich.

"When Nana got cursed..." Beryl begins.

"When she *thought* she got cursed," Pearl interrupts.

"Why did she walk all the way to Broome when she could have jumped off the cliffs around here?"

"She had to," Pearl replies.

165

"Why?"

Pearl points to the cave confrontation in the mural where Great-Grandma Pearl painted the future before she was sent off in disgrace by the elder.

"Because she saw me, jumping off the cliffs in Broome to save her. I thought it was her painting me jumping off the cliff at the caravan park," Pearl says, pointing at the beginning, "but it wasn't."

Beryl turns in her chair to look at Pearl with her good eye.

"So, if you didn't jump in after her when she got to Broome, none of us would have been born?"

Pearl beams and hugs her, saying, "Exactly!"

Marnie enviously looks upon their easy love and mutters, "Yeah, well if she didn't see you jumping off those cliffs, she never would have gotten in trouble in the first place, my girl. But it's a good thing that you did, saving the roadhouse."

The sugar-coated pill, Pearl thinks. At least she appreciates it.

"Too right," Beryl agrees with Marnie. "How can we ever thank you?"

"I'm sorry I was so tough on you, kiddo," Yanush says, taking a big gulp of vodka. "Then you turned around and saved our bacon. They don't make 'em any better than that," he adds, saluting Pearl with his glass, but staring at Marnie.

"Just lucky Massimo loved my paintings," Pearl replies. "I went back and threw that bloody shark tooth at the elder in the cave vision, but it didn't fix anything," she adds.

"Weren't you scared?" Beryl asks.

Pearl shakes her head. "Mad. I was so wild about what he did to her that I wanted to kill him, but he was already dead!"

They all laugh like jackals and cannot stop for ages. It's the rare sort of laughter that saves them when their lives can't get any tougher, but, somehow, they survive.

When they settle down, Beryl wipes a tear of laughter from her cheek and goes over to the mural, tenderly touches her nana in the nearby cave and returns to Pearl.

"If you can do it, so can I. I've got to see… if I can help people."

"Bravo," Yanush says, moving to hug her. "Your good eye will stay safe now, Bubba."

"Not me," Marnie puts in. "I've got a job to get back to and I see fine," she adds, glancing at Beryl. She points at the bath section. "Wasn't as scared as you were that day, 'eh, little sis?" She juts her chin at Pearl. "Wasn't me your hand went through! I was just hopping mad at Mum for scatchin' my face."

While Bubba and Bear are caught up in their hug, Marnie quietly asks Pearl, "Are you coming back with me on the bus when my holiday time's up? I've missed you."

Pearl warms to being asked, but going back feels like a backward step that she's grown past taking. She shakes her head, touching Marnie's arm as she answers, "Thanks, Mum, but I've got to stay. Maybe they can live on the dole or the pension when they're old enough, but Aunty needs my support now if she wants to help people. And I can't go back until we find Dad."

Marnie nods, which doesn't make losing her prick of a husband and this wonderful new change in her only daughter hurt any less.

Chapter Seventeen

They're all there, when Pearl wakes late and wanders into the roadhouse: Norm, Ray and Juno, Pat and Davo, all eating a breakfast of pancakes that Yanush has made them.

"Gidday, Pearl," they say in unison.

Marnie pulls out a chair so Pearl can sit between herself and Beryl. Yanush hands Pearl a plate of pancakes and pushes the maple syrup bottle toward her.

Pearl feels warm and wonderful in her heart. This is what she's missed: family. They all feel like family now, this loving crew of old misfits, except for Juno, who looks pretty young. She wonders when the best time would be to tell Mum and Aunty about Marlon and Charlie, their Indigenous family, including the Women of the Shark Dreaming, who might already be on their way.

"Sleep well?" Ray asks.

"Yep," Pearl replies. "Hey, Norm, have you got any spare glass lying about?"

"Plenty."

"I was thinking about the family photos we took down," Pearl says, glancing at Beryl. "Can't leave them stashed in the caravan. They'd look cool under glass on these tables so everyone could see the real people in the mural."

Beryl and Yanush nod to each other, while Marnie tries to remember... which photos? She isn't sure that she's ready to see herself in a photo with Red yet, back when they used to live here.

"Great idea!" Ray replies. "We've got a glass cutter on the heap somewhere... Ah luv, I mean Pearl, we reckon Juno here's been missing his necklace and some answers," he says, putting an arm around Juno's shoulder, who's busy pushing the maple syrup aside to reach the bottle of soy sauce in the middle of the table.

Pearl glances at Aunty, who's looking unsettled by the idea, as is Marnie.

"I was wondering who that belongs to," Pat says, pointing at the gold pagoda necklace still lying in the bottom of the tank.

"You do it," Aunty mutters to Pearl, who isn't going to let her off that easily.

"Leave it with us," Pearl tells Ray. "We might have some answers by the time you get back with the glass."

"*Arigato*," Juno says, putting his hands together with a nod of gratitude, knowing that they are talking about him because Ray said his name and Pat pointed at his necklace. He doesn't know why Ray made him practice putting his necklace in the bottom of the empty fish tank when it was at Country Downs. He is just happy to have pleased them by doing that – a small price to pay for their hospitality. He doesn't understand why the artist left it in the bottom of her filled up fish tank and ignored it after all that practice. Very strange Australian custom, storing gold in fish tanks. Everybody in Japan knows that it is fish that bring luck, prosperity and good fortune.

"Gotta see that," Davo reckons, having missed out on seeing Pearl's 'tank pranks', as Norm and Ray used to call them, even though neither of them or Marnie have seen it, either.

"There's nuthin' to see," Beryl replies. "Just Pearl with her face in the fish tank. She does all the seeing."

"You can, too," Pearl tells her. "And you," she says to Marnie, whose face immediately closes shop.

"Nah, nah," Beryl replies, "Not with all these jokers looking on."

"You heard the lady," Yanush says, rising to clear away the plates. "She's not a performing seal."

Norm pushes his chair back and Ray follows suit.

Juno sees them rising and stands.

"Thanks for the pancakes," Norm says, picking up his keys.

"Got a tape measure?" Davo asks Yanush, as he rolls his wheelchair back.

Yanush grabs one from the kitchen drawer and starts measuring up one of the identical dining tables.

"I'm so glad you're better," Pat tells Beryl, patting her back as she wheels Davo past. "See you when we get back."

"Wanna help me bring in the photos?" Pearl asks her mum as she heads out.

Marnie follows her out to the caravan.

*

The photos are spread between the tables still in their frames when Beryl comes out of the Ladies with a towel over her shoulder.

"Let's get this Juno thing done before everyone gets back," she says.

She starts nervously rubbing her hair with the towel, then thinks better of it. Not much point if she's gunna stick her head in the fish tank. "I haven't opened my eyes in water since we nearly drowned," she admits, casting a hand at that part of the mural.

"Me either," Marnie says, wincing at the very thought of it.

"Was bad enough with the eye drops, but I blinked them out quick smart," Beryl admits.

"How about I start?" Pearl offers. "And I won't tell ya what I see, then you have a go and we'll compare notes?"

"What if it's bad?" Beryl asks. "What do we know about this guy?"

"Nothing," Pearl replies, crossing the floor to stand by the fish tank. "But whatever sent him cycling across the Nullarbor, that's what we'll see. Watch, you two. All I do is take a deep breath and stick my head in with my eyes open." She turns to Beryl. "If you get scared, pull your head out, or raise your hand and we'll pull you out."

Beryl nods, asking shakily, "Do I have to swim in there?"

"Not proper swimming, just do bird-frog," Pearl says, demonstrating big bird arms in mid-air and sitting to show Beryl her frog-kicks.

"Easier said than done," Marnie mutters. "You must be out of your bloody mind."

"Shuddup," Beryl says, concentrating hard on watching Pearl in action.

Pearl takes a big breath, pushes her face into the tank and is immediately assailed by the sound of a loud TV compere speaking excitedly in Japanese, introducing contestant "Juno", as she rises in a lake vision.

She resurfaces inside a game show being filmed at a lake, which is lined with an excited, young, Japanese audience. Juno, dressed in a bright yellow onesie and matching crash helmet, must ride over the lake on a lit-up, golden path and reach the golden pagoda to win the game. The path violently heaves, bucking Juno and his bicycle straight off it into the lake, prompting yelling from the compere and uncontrollable laughter from the audience.

Pearl checks below the surface of the lake and confirms that it is their Juno.

His expression is crushed, after such a shamefully short performance.

As he rises and hauls his gold tinsel-adorned pushbike out of the lake, Pearl lifts her head out of the vision.

Inhaling deeply, Pearl accepts Aunty's towel and exhales, saying, "Not too bad. Your turn."

Beryl leans over the tank water and hesitates. She straightens, takes out her glass eye and hands it to Marnie.

The eye in her palm stares up at irked Marnie as Beryl takes a huge breath, grips the glass on each side and pushes all of her face into the tank.

Aunty's good eye is open, moving from side to side, seeing. Pearl smiles.

Beryl grabs the necklace and rises in no time, panting and looking chuffed that she did it.

"What did you see?" Pearl asks, handing her back the towel.

Marnie gives back the glass eye.

"Poor little bugger would have felt better if he got further, but falling off right away like that publicly humiliated him," Beryl responds, pocketing the necklace, drying her face, and popping the eye back in.

Pearl jumps up and down excitedly yelling, "You did it! You did it, Aunty! On your first go, too!"

Beryl succumbs to a little dance on the spot with Pearl and halts. "It's one thing seeing stuff, but how do we talk to him about it if he can't speak English?"

"I thought of that," Marnie mutters, "but neither of you would have listened. What happened to him?"

"Lost his confidence trying to ride his bike in a booby-trapped, Japanese game show," Beryl responds sadly. "Fell in a lake and got humiliated."

"Spot on, Aunty!" Pearl says, trying to think of a way to assist him. "He likely set his own challenge, riding across the Nullarbor, and would have aced it, if Norm and Ray hadn't plucked him off the side of the road."

"Hard one," Marnie reckons.

"Maybe him coming to another country and biking such a distance is all to avoid facing the folk back home?" Beryl suggests.

"Now you're talking!" Pearl exclaims, impressed by Beryl's intuition.

Now that Pearl has their full attention, she decides it's the right time to tell them. "Um, Aunty, Mum, we're expecting visitors."

*

Just as Pearl, Marnie and Beryl finish arranging the now unframed photos on the dining room tables, ready for the glass tops, there's a quiet knock on the glass front of the roadhouse.

The women look up and see a group of old Indigenous women, wearing a riot of colours and a sea of smiles, with their hands cupped against the glass, all peering at the mural, looking impressed by Pearl's work.

"They're here," Pearl tells her mum and aunty, who both look

172

awkward, particularly Marnie, who scowls as Pearl rushes out to greet them.

"Hello," she says. "I'm Pearl. Are you the… Women of the Shark Dreaming?"

"We sure are," answers the oldest one, who's wearing an 'Always Was Always Will Be Aboriginal Land' hand-painted slogan on her t-shirt. "Charlie sent us. I'm Violet, this is Cindy, Hazel, Doris and Gloria. We're artists, too, but we don't paint like that."

"Welcome, artists," Pearl replies, ushering them in through the fly strips.

"Aunties," Cindy says. "Call us aunties."

Inside, Beryl and Marnie stand up, at a loss for words.

Pearl introduces them, "This is my mum, Marnie, and my Aunty Beryl. And this is my great-grandma, Pearl," she adds, pointing her out in the cave section.

The old women take immediate interest and go straight to that part of the mural.

"We know this story," Violet says, wondering when to tell them that her real name wasn't Pearl.

"He got a hiding for that," Hazel puts in, which makes the others chuckle, breaking the ice.

"Yeah, I know," Pearl replies. "Who wants a cuppa?"

All hands go up.

*

On Norm's veranda, littered with sawhorse trundle tables and glass in various sizes, the crew are enjoying their smoko of beer and biltong.

Yanush asks Norm and Ray, "Have you heard from Eddie?"

"Nup," Ray replies, "Bugger's dropped off the radar."

"He'll be back soon enough," Norm puts in. "Probably just working out of range."

"How about you two?" Yanush asks Pat and Davo.

"I tried his mobile when we were Perth side," Davo says. "Went straight to message bank."

"Me too," Yanush sighs. "I left a message, but he might not get it for a while. You've all seen the mural. He *has* to tell Pearl where to find Red's remains."

"True, yeah, reckon," they chorus.

"So, if any of you hear from him, let me know," Yanush adds.

"Yep, too right, for sure," they chorus again, between swigs of beer.

"Big shock for Marnie, finding out that way," Pat puts in. "Worse for Pearl."

"Unlike Eddie not to man up and tell her," Norm says. "He must have had his reasons."

"How he could just leave Red's corpse rotting out there is beyond me," Davo adds, screwing up his nose.

"Guilt about the nugget?" Norm suggests, feeling guilty himself for drunkenly trying to put Eddie off Pearl in no uncertain terms when he was pissed off with her, and Ray.

"Yeah maybe," Ray replies, "But he gave that nugget to Pearl, so at least she can use it to pay for Red's funeral… if she finds him."

"I'd like to be a fly on the wall if Marnie gets a hold of him," Pat puts in. "She'll rip him to shreds if he doesn't cough up."

Bonox walks over twitching his ears like he's eavesdropping on this gossip.

Juno goes over to pat him.

"You're a bull, Bonox," Norm tells him.

"Thinks he's human," Ray agrees.

*

Back at the roadhouse, the Women of the Shark Dreaming can't look at the tabletop photos of their deceased relatives, but do look at the mural to work out their blood lines and skin groups.

Discovering that they are all 'sharks', related by this *boodya* county, place of their birth, doesn't sit comfortably with Marnie. She's still offside with Joe the elder for ousting her nana from their tribe in the first place.

"That prick cursed her with his shark tooth," Marnie mutters, "no matter what anyone says about him being sorry for it."

Violet takes it upon her herself to be the first to try to clear up that misunderstanding. "It's like this," she begins, pointing at the elder. "Shark was Joe's personal totem as well as his birthplace totem. It means that he protected sharks and didn't hunt or eat 'em."

Hazel pipes up, "And he was given that totem at birth when he was smoked by his elder, because his elder could see that he'd be like a shark, brave, fearless, lean, strong."

"And deadly," Cindy puts in, forgetting herself about the bad thing he did that day.

Beryl gives her a look, wondering which sort of 'deadly' she's referring to.

"Violet's an elder," Cindy blabs. "She smokes the baby girls to see what their totem is."

Pearl, Beryl and Marnie stare in discomfort, all trying to work out how they 'smoke' babies.

Noticing, Doris speaks up for the first time, saying, "Joe would have had a deadly focus like a shark, but even he couldn't make a shark do anything."

Cindy goes over to the part of the mural where the Tiger Shark is taking Great-Grandma Pearl.

"There's no pet sharks, even if they're your totem," she says. "If you cross their domain, wrong place wrong time."

Hazel picks up the thread, "The sea is like the land to them. They belong to it, and they hunt in it. Joe couldn't cause that," she tells Marnie. "But if your nana *believed* that he could, the power of her belief might have attracted the shark to her."

"So, it was *her* fault?" Marnie spits out, making eyes at Beryl and Pearl, muttering, "As if."

"Joe wasn't a proper *warra*, bad man," Gloria tells Marnie. "That shark tooth he threw was just him using something to scare her out of jumping off the cliffs, because that's what he thought she painted, without permission." With a dismissive flick of the wrist, she adds, "He didn't understand." To Pearl, Beryl and Marnie, she states, "Men don't know women's business."

To Marnie, Violet reveals, "Your Nana Pearl's birth name was Kalinda… meaning seer. She had different learning to his. In our culture, a man cannot chuck *marbun* at a woman," she further reveals, "which is why he got a hiding from the women."

"Mum always said we were cursed," Marnie states, crossing her arms, "and we never knew Nana as Kalinda."

Beryl thinks about it, then says, "She wouldn't have spoken English when she got dragged on to that lugger. Peter Pearler likely called her Pearl."

Pearl nods, a little sad to have lost their same name connection, but the seer part she likes.

Beryl continues, "Grandma Pearl, Kalinda, you say, would have told Peter Pearler what happened that day. He warned Mum to stay away from blackfellas, even though she wanted to come back here to her mum's country, as far from sharks as she could get."

The old women nod, beginning to understand why these three have been away from their culture for so long, all likely angry and pushing people away because of it, too.

"Why Nana wanted Peter Pearler to string that shark tooth in the middle of the necklace he made her is beyond me," Marnie scowls. "I always hated that shark tooth."

"It gave me the heebie-jeebies, too," Beryl agrees.

Hazel frowns, sorry to hear that, "Shark's your birthplace totem, sis," she tells Marnie, fingering the shark tooth in her bracelet. "No good hating yourself. Don't be ashamed."

Marnie doesn't, until she glances at Beryl, who's giving Pearl a tiny nod of agreement about it doing her no good to hate herself.

"Knock it off, you two!" Marnie flares, raising her lighter with a cigarette between her teeth.

"Do you think their nana believed it was *marbun*?" Cindy quietly asks Violet.

"*Marbun* can be curse or black magic," Violet replies. "If she *thought* he was chucking *marbun* at her when he sent her off, she *thought* she was cursed."

"I saw it," Pearl weighs in. "The only word she asked was *marbun. And* he didn't answer."

"Charlie might have told you, Joe was sorry for that," Violet replies, "because he thought he accidentally sent her to her death. He got payback in his lifetime, but the shame got passed down. Charlie says it's a good thing that you set that story straight, Bub, about her not dying, at least not right away."

An uneasy quiet descends, which doesn't last long.

"There's saltwater people up north," Violet confides. "Shark whisperers some say. They're *bolya gadak*, shaman keepers of the stone of the shark. *Yanyuwa*, their shark language, is almost forgotten now. Only a handful of old people still speak it. Maybe they could help."

"See here?" she says, pointing to the spirit of Kalinda in the sea cave at the beginning. "Water is what connects us. They might say your ancestor was like Moondo, ghost of the sea white shark in their dreaming. She was a powerful pathfinder-healer, just like you, Pearl."

Beryl and Marnie look at Pearl. They cannot deny that they all see in water, but Pearl's been the fearless one, using it to work out their story, despite their dire warnings, and it seems to be helping, not only them, either.

"One thing's for sure. Seers can fix *anything*, and you three come from a line of healers.

None of us have your power of sight," Violet admits, admiringly... "I have to ask my elders about who can come next to help you with that special learning. Might be the Saltwater People," she tells Pearl, "or a medicine woman from Broome, 'cause you say your nana was born in Broome," she tells Beryl and Marnie, then returns to Pearl. "Even without your permission, your great-grandma painted..."

The other old women shift uncomfortably in their seats, muttering, "Wrong way, really wrong way."

Violet points again to the spirit in the sea cave, telling Pearl, "Kalinda gave you her strength and passed on her knowledge the only way she could." She glances at the others, adding,

"Wrong way for sure, but she was young, and her learning was not complete."

The old women nod sorrowfully. They see in Pearl's great-grandma and her daughter, Raeleen, all First Nations people who got disconnected from their culture, never to return. They're here sharing stories because they believe if anything can heal these women and bring them back to culture it's their family, their country, and their learning.

"Whoever comes here next," Violet says, still seeing resistance in Marnie, "will need your permission, left eye to left eye, to blow off that shark trauma and replace it with healing."

Beryl and Pearl look receptive as she continues, "The learning takes a lifetime and you're already far behind. You even missed out on being smoked when you were bubs to find out your animal totems. Who wants to get smoked?"

"I already know mine," Pearl says, crossing her arms.

"Don't be like that, Bub," Violet replies, thinking Pearl knows a lot for a no culture kid, but she still has to make a proper start.

"I do!" Beryl volunteers, pointing to her good left eye. "I give my permission."

"Not me," Marnie mutters, lighting another cigarette.

"Marnie's been smoking since birth," Beryl says. "Go on, chicken! Marnie's a chicken!"

"Bush turkey," Pearl chips in, elbowing her mum.

The old women cackle, which soon makes everyone crack up, even Marnie, because such silly, healing laughter has been in short supply.

*

By the time Pat and the men return with the glass tabletops at dusk, they find all the photos laid out ready on the tables, but the women are nowhere to be seen.

"Bubba," Yanush calls in the kitchen and in their room, but she's not there.

"Pearl," Norm calls out the back, but there's no answer. Ray heads inside to put a letter for Pearl from Massimo on the servery bench in case he forgets.

Norm sees smoke way down the back where Bubba and Bear used to have campfire nights. He shades his eyes from the setting sun, squints and just makes out Pearl and Beryl sitting in a circle of Indigenous women, looking ashen faced and wearing fur head bands.

All the women are gazing upon Marnie in the centre of the circle, the last to be smoked. She leans over smoking Emu Bush branches, while Violet rubs her face with ash.

"Come and see *this!*" Norm yells inside to the others.

"Don't disturb them," Pat cautions, as she wheels Davo out, just far enough to see.

Davo pushes his sunnies on top of his head, saying, "Looks like women's business to me."

Yanush starts walking toward them, but Pat grabs his arm.

"What are they doing?" he asks, concerned about all that smoke getting in Beryl's good eye.

"I've seen that on Groote Island," Davo replies, "when I was working up north on the prawn trawlers. Usually it's the babies they smoke, to work out their animal totems."

The Women of the Shark Dreaming start dancing, circling each other, stamping their bare feet, and moving like sharks. The sound of their singing rises, along with the rhythm of their clap sticks.

Violet reaches for Pearl and Beryl. They get up and join Marnie in the centre, who's trying to escape and sit down, but Pearl holds her hand. The trio are clumsy at first, but soon get the hang of doing the shark dance.

"Wow!" Pat says, sorry that she's not Indigenous or she'd rush over to join in. "Go gals!"

"This calls for a barbeque!" Yanush announces, heading inside to prepare it.

Chapter Eighteen

After the barbeque, when all the thanks, goodbyes and please come back any time are sincerely said to the Women of the Shark Dreaming, the roadhouse community takes stock.

Davo jokes with Beryl, "So, you black chicks know your totem animals now?"

"Yep, Pearl was right!" Beryl replies. "She's an eagle, I'm a wombat and Marnie's an echidna."

Beryl smiles inwardly about how right Violet was because Pearl's direct and fearless, she's slow and round-about by nature and Marnie's spiky. She approaches Juno, holding up his pagoda necklace, saying, "This is Japan." She makes flying arms as she continues, "You must fly home soon to Japan."

Juno nods, relieved, glancing at Norm and Ray, surprised to be accepting his necklace back and happy that he will not have to stay here longer. He immediately gives the necklace to Ray with a bow, hoping that they will understand that he wants them to have it because he no longer needs it. He bought the gold pagoda necklace as a good luck charm before competing in the game show, and it brought him no luck. Juno cannot believe how fast he flew here to escape the shame and humiliation he suffered in that competition, boarding the first flight from Japan, hiding behind his desert challenge. He realises that he no longer needs that, either.

It is the kindness and generosity of this odd couple, who have shared their broken-down property and inedible meals with him, while living in a shameless junk heap, that has healed Juno. After a stint at Country Downs, he no longer needs to prove himself to anybody, and, besides, he misses his family and knows they must be missing him too. He hopes that his bicycle and saddle bags will be a welcome addition to Norm's junk heap.

"*Arigato*, Juno," Ray says, putting on the pagoda necklace

with a little bow. "Did you see him going home, Beryl, or was that you, Pearl shame-shifter?" Ray says, a bit miffed that they will soon be losing their first and maybe only Country Downs guest.

He hands Pearl the letter he left on the bench, thinking that Massimo never said goodbye or wrote to him.

"We both looked in the tank," Pearl replies, distracted by the handwriting on the front which says 'Pearl Oracle' and the roadhouse's address.

She flips it over, smiling as she reads 'Massimo Free Man Venuti from Venezia' as the sender, with his new address on the back. She pushes the letter into the bib of her overalls.

"Bravo! You did it, Bubba," Yanush is saying, looking proudly at Beryl.

"Mum, can you take Juno to Perth on the bus with you when you go?" Pearl asks, "and make sure he catches a plane back to Japan?"

Marnie nods, "Yeah. I might as well do my bit, since you two are."

Beryl and Pearl give Marnie a hug. She stiffly suffers their embrace at first and slowly melts into them when they do not let her go.

*

Once all have left or gone to bed, Pearl pensively sits by the tank, pleased that most of her family mysteries are solved now, assisted by Massimo's generosity in allowing them to stay. She feels humbled, like a detective whose deductions solved a few mysteries, but others had to come to help her solve her own. And more will come, with her permission.

Pearl reminds herself that she didn't need permission to paint the mural. It was just her weird trance way of connecting with her ancestor, in response to being swum through – also without permission – just in time, too. The learning may never end, but it's already gone a long way toward healing her heart and Aunty's. Mum's, too – especially Mum's.

Pearl pulls out Massimo's letter and opens it.

"*Perla mia,*" he writes, "I hope you are well. I came home and decided that I cannot stay married with Cassandra, so we are getting a divorce. I am going to this gathering of amazing people in June. Will you join me? Australia taught me that it's the people not the forgotten places and these people are your tribe, *Perla*. I will pay for all if you are coming, including your own room. *Baci,* Massimo."

Pearl unfolds a flyer from The Shamanic Society advertising a once in a lifetime retreat in the high Andes of Peru. 'Engage in traditional ceremonies and learn shamanic wisdom from Peruvian *Maestros* and Indigenous shamans from around the world. Join us on a path of harmony, unifying body, soul, and personal growth. 'Together We Will Heal the World.'

Tall order, healing the world, Pearl thinks as she folds the flyer, curious about why Massimo thinks they're 'her tribe'. Because they're Indigenous? Her tribe just found her…

Now that Pearl knows she belongs to this Nullarbor country and that her *boodya* is not some 'forgotten place' of Massimo's imagination, she wants to stay awhile and learn more. And there are no forgotten places in First Nations' culture – that much she knows. It's all about remembering, honouring, and belonging to country, so different to being the family's shame-buster and shock-absorber hoping to paint her way to contentment and connection.

She hasn't worked out how to belong in those two worlds yet, let alone this third mob in Peru! If she read that flyer last year, she would have laughed and binned it.

Now, she pockets it, softly sighing, "Kalinda, Kalinda, Kalinda."

Pearl hasn't forgotten that Massimo was the only one who recognised the 'oracle' in her from the beginning. The more Pearl knows, the less she knows she knows…

What's a shaman, anyway?

Pity it isn't a tribe of *seers*, she thinks, but she can find them in the next room! She chuckles as she heads for bed, deciding to worry about Peru later.

*

A while later, Eddie pulls up at the roadhouse, staring gobsmacked out of his windscreen as the full impact of the renovations hits him. The mural is illuminated behind glass like a fish tank in the desert. He doesn't notice Beryl and Yanush's old sedan parked behind their caravan. Full of trepidation, he eases out of his ute, holding a bag of water with a pair of goldfish in it.

"Pearl," he calls quietly, but nobody answers.

He walks into the roadhouse and gently floats the goldfish bag on the surface of the tank water. Eddie stands back from the mural to fully take it in, emitting a low whistle. He frowns on himself for stealing the nugget, but looks well upon the ending, where he makes his peace with Big Red.

Eddie looks around again, heads out the back and knocks on Pearl's bedroom door, calling, "Pearl. Are you there, Pearl?" louder this time.

No answer. Eddie heads back into the roadhouse, aware that it's late, but it was a long drive from the Ceduna Aquarium, and he didn't want to arrive empty-handed.

A fly is zapped with a sharp crack by the electric fly zapper hanging from the ceiling.

Eddie spins around, comes face to face with Pearl and her great-grandma in the mural and turns back. His gaze settles on the top-lit fish tank.

"Nah," he mutters, listening to the surface of the water.

All he can hear is the overhead fan revolving too slowly and the fish rustling in their plastic bag, floating on the surface.

The clock ticks.

Eddie grips the sides of the tank. Knuckles white, teeth clenched, he takes a huge breath and pushes his whole face into the tank.

The toilet flushes. Pearl emerges from the Ladies in her long strawberry t-shirt, sees Eddie doubled over with his head in the fish tank and stops.

Eddie yells underwater, in a burst of bubbles, "*Peeeeeaaarrrlll!*"

Pearl's eyes widen with amusement. She creeps over and slaps the side of the tank. Eddie rears back gasping, blowing water which runs down his shirt.

"Whatcha doin', Eddie?" Pearl asks.

"Lookin' for you."

Eddie sees new softness in Pearl's gaze, a sort of yielding in her that he finds irresistible.

"Got ya something," he manages to say.

He indicates the pair of goldfish floating in their plastic bag, who goggle up at delighted Pearl, wagging their tails as she leans over to look at them. She smiles her thanks to hunkalicious Eddie through the fish tank, the grounded guy with only one secret, which she found room in her heart to forgive.

"I wanted to break the windmill," she straightens to say. "Like you said. It was all I could think of to get you back… here."

Silence expands all around them as they gaze at each other over the top-lit fish tank.

"*Did* you?" Eddie replies with the faintest of smiles as he rounds the tank.

Pearl looks evenly up into his eyes, asking, "Will you take me to Dad? He deserves a proper burial."

"Of course," Eddie replies, relieved to be given this chance to redeem himself. "I was going to offer. I did bury him."

"Yeah, thought so. I mean a proper funeral," Pearl says. "Mum's here."

"I'll take you both," Eddie sombrely replies.

Pearl nods, feeling a bit worried about Marnie and Eddie being in the same room.

"Some blackfella rellies came 'round," she confides. "Amazing people. They helped us sort out a terrible misunderstanding and reconnected us to this place."

Eddie nods, pleased to hear Pearl sounding lighter, relieved of some of the hurt she's been carrying. He's done repairs on himself, too, he thinks, by making his peace with Red and burying him, and revisiting the beach where his mum suicided, to apologise to her. It's been hard to forgive himself for calling her nuts, when she said she wanted to swim out and not back, and then being too late to save her.

Eddie blinks back a tear. Will the wake from her swimming feet never stop splashing salt water in his eyes? He accepts that some things take longer to mend.

Pearl dashes away her own tear. It feels *so good* to be found, but family starts at home, and she still cringes about all the lip and pain her old, angry self dished up to Marnie before she left.

"I'd just busted up with Mum so bad when I met you," she says in barely a whisper, "but she's here now, and we've made up."

"It's how we make up that matters," Eddie replies, "if we can forgive ourselves. Only you could have taught me that, Pearl."

Pearl feels so grateful for this that she comes right out and says it, "I'm sorry I kept pushing you away, Eddie... I've really missed you."

Eddie gently takes Pearl's face in his hands and kisses her. The goldfish twirl delightedly around each other in their bag.

For the first time, Pearl feels safe in a guy's embrace, like she never wants this kiss to end, which is how she knows that this is not the end of something wonderful, but the beginning.

Printed in Great Britain
by Amazon

52180022R00110